Small town antichrist

(a scots armageddon)

Small town antichrist

(a scots armageddon)

Iain Grant

First published in 1999 by
Oil of the Greater North Limited
PO Box 232
York YO1 2SY

email:oilpress@btinternet.com

A CIP catalogue record for this book is available
from the British Library

ISBN 0 9533495 0 0

Trade distribution by
Signature Book Representation Ltd, Manchester
Tel: 0161 834 8767

Typeset in Bembo and Helvetica by
Palimpsest Book Production Limited,
Polmont, Stirlingshire
Printed in England by Redwood Books Ltd, London

Small town antichrist

(a scots armageddon)

GENESIS

In the beginning.

Let me start at the beginning.

The first word.

In the beginning was the word.

Let there be Light.

Let me cast Light on what was dark.

Damn. Damn, damn, damn, damn, damn.

This will never work. Look, we'll do this stuff later. Let's start with where I realised who I really was. Who I really was. The 'who' has a capital W.

REVELATION

It was the fourth time that I'd been told I was the Antichrist.

Am I going too fast for you, or can you keep up?

Good. Write this down then.

It was the fourth time I'd been told I was the antichrist. That's capital A, Antichrist. It was at a party, and the person who told me was some Californian girlie who was reading everybody's auras. She was drivelling on about people having sensitive natures. She told one guy he had an artistic soul, but that he should get in touch with his feelings, otherwise he would never be able to express his inner self properly. Then she came to me. She looked me in the eye, went white and ran out of the room screaming.

One person laughed, then there was an uncomfortable silence. A friend of the Californian girlie looked at me as if I'd done something terrible, then went after her. The conversation started again, then stopped abruptly a few minutes later when the girlie and her pal came back into the room. The girlie pointed at me and said 'And thou shalt know him for he shall bear the Mark of the Beast. He is the Evil One' and left.

Somebody said well, that's something you don't see every day, nodded at me and said that it was a pleasure to meet someone interesting for a change, O Mighty Lord of Darkness. There was some nervous laughter, and the ice broke. I was the toast of the party. People approached and begged me to destroy their enemies or grant them untold wealth in exchange for their souls. I got off with some English girlie and shagged her in the downstairs toilet.

MY MASTER'S VOICE

What happened at the party was kind of a joke, but to me it was also a kind of revelation. Things which had happened began to make sense. I saw myself in a new light, and understood myself.

There had always been this capital-vee Voice in my head. Make sure you write that with a capital. Some people have voices which say 'Poor man, give him a tenner, I wish I could do something for him' or 'Ah, what a cute baby, and how happy the mother looks, what a picture of contentment'. What my voice always said was 'Wouldn't it be funny to kick him in the nuts' or 'push her under the train'. Sometimes, on a Thursday afternoon when I was stuck in the office, my Voice would shout and scream in my head 'Destroy it all. Destroy. Destroy'. My Voice would then show me visions of my colleagues engulfed in flames, burning to death in agony and leaping from the highest window to escape the fire. I would smile at the thought.

I had attached no particular significance to the Voice, though. I had thought it perfectly normal. I had thought that everyone has a voice. Until the party.

Now I know that everyone has a voice, and all of them listen. But I also know that my Voice is different from theirs. Their voices are their own petty human voices, their jealousy, their fear, their frustration, their ambition. My Voice is the Voice of my Father. My Voice is the reason I shall triumph. My Voice speaks to me constantly. It says 'It's going to get worse'.

A DATE WITH DESTINY

This party, the one where I was capital-r Revealed to myself, was the first social event I'd been to for a long time. I'd been hibernating since my wife died.

Now I was Revealed, I understood that what had happened, the capital-a Accident, had been capital-n Necessary.

Look, there are a lot of capitals in this and I can't keep telling you every single time. Tell you what – when there's a capital I'll put my arms out like this. If you're not looking I'll whack you on the head. OK? Now, write, cabbageface.

Sorry, Cabbageface.

I understood that what had happened, the Accident, good, well done, very observant, I'm glad you're paying attention, I understood that what had happened, the Accident, had been Necessary. It was part of being prepared to learn of my True Nature. Her death was Necessary for my Evil Nature to be fully realised. She died for My Sins.

It is strange, now that I reflect on it in full knowledge of my True Nature, how reluctant I had been to go to the party. I almost rang to say I had a cold, make some excuse, say that my Uncle Wilf had had to go into hospital for emergency urology and I had to look after his cockatiel. And yet I felt strangely compelled to go, despite my inner emptiness. I can see this now as the workings of my Destiny.

HUMDRUM EXISTENCE

I should tell you a bit about myself as I had been before I was Revealed, so that you can see that there was nothing special about me on the outside. Evil lurks where you least expect it.

Ordinary, that is the word you might use to describe the life we led. Or humdrum. I like that word – hum is like the buzzing of flies, and drum could be war drums, but the word itself is so humdrum. It symbolises hidden depths beneath an outward appearance of nothing very special.

In the beginning was the word, and the word was that it was humdrum.

I worked in the Scottish Office in a senior administrative

capacity. I still do. It is not a job I enjoy, especially, but I am good at it and it seems to suit me, temperamentally. I have always felt an inner need to promote the interests and meet the needs of the people of Scotland.

I had a wife, as you know, two cats, a nice house in an exclusive Edinburgh street and a car called Henry. The house was, why am I using the past tense, it still is, a large Georgian thing. Four storeys, six bedrooms. It was my parents'. It's in Regent Terrace, on the rather swanky Calton Hill, next door to the American Consulate. I've been its owner since I was 14.

Edinburgh was the centre of my life. I had a hard childhood and adolescence, but I found the city a great consolation. People of the right sort can have a great life here. Edinburgh has everything you could possibly need. It has beauty, it is the country's centre of power and social life, and is the one place where everything that is even remotely of interest happens.

Calling the car Henry was my wife's idea. I thought it foolish to call a car anything other than 'the car', but she insisted, so I humoured her. She thought it was, as she said, 'cute'. It was my opinion, and this was one of the few disagreements we ever had, that if you were going to call a Volvo estate anything, you should give it a more refined name. Torquil, Cameron. That sort of thing.

She was subject to fits of whimsy though. She was not methodical. It was part of her charm. She would wander off into abstract speculations about our future, and she would put tins of food onto shelves in a totally random fashion. She always left it to me to alphabetise them.

She wanted children, but we never had them. Hence the cats, Chip and Dale. We thought one of us, maybe both, was infertile. I wasn't bothered, but she was. I did maintain that our childlessness was at least in part due to her being so disorganised. She never knew where she was in her menstrual cycle. I had to keep a diary for her.

She said she was happy.

I thought I was, but I wasn't.

SOME PORTENTS OF MY DESTINY

I did not embark on my career in Evil until I had already led as rewarding a conventional life as it is possible to lead. This was part of my Destiny. I had to understand the common herd if I were to rule over them in my Father's name.

This is not to say that there were no indications of my Destiny in my childhood. My followers will say that I showed one or two early signs. I was, for instance, a disruptive presence in Sunday School, and used to argue with my so-called teachers constantly, but I never had anything very constructive to say. They used to make me sharpen pencils to keep me out of the way.

It is also true that I was once arrested for stamping on pigeons in the High Street. I was 14. I see this as no more than a youthful peccadillo. Worse things happen in Edinburgh drawing rooms every day of the year. Especially on Calton Hill. Besides which, I had only stamped on five before the policeman came, dragged along by some horrified old bastard who could neither see the funny side of the way a pigeon sort of explodes if you jump on it just right, or appreciate the skill and cunning which went into it. You have to catch them unawares. They can move surprisingly quickly, even without flying, and you have to catch them with a lot of force if you are to make them burst, rather than merely kill them. It involves sneaking up on them, not alarming them, and then leaping on them from as high as you can manage, whilst bearing in mind the need for stealth. It's a very difficult balance to achieve, and I remember thinking at the time that some recognition of the skills I had shown wouldn't have gone amiss. It would have been better than all the hoo-ha of the court appearance and the stories in the newspaper.

I was a gloomy child. I had a lot to be gloomy about. There was my parents, for one thing. And their deaths, for another. Still, it was going to get worse.

ABOUT THIS BOOK

It occurs to me I ought also to say why I am writing this book. Dictating it★, to be strictly accurate, but it amounts to pretty much the same thing. It is the Grocer of Doom who is doing the actual writing with pen and paper thing. I can't be bothered with anything that menial. The Grocer is my slave. He is a minor character in my story, and you will hear about him later. A little. Unless I decide to eliminate him altogether. To expunge him from my memory.

★ I could also, it occurs to me, have caused it to be set down by the Power of my Will, but there is a greater degree of exactitude in having the setting-down done oneself. Much of what I have to say, given my concerns about interpretation, has to be formulated precisely. Also, other things might occur to me later on, and I can come back and change my mind.

Ouch

My Memory.

That's better.

I am writing this book

What is it now?

No, I don't want you to write book with a capital B. Not yet, anyway, as we've only just started, and it would look silly, like we had too grand an idea of what we were doing. Maybe later. Now please stop interrupting. Pay attention to my voice and to the hand-signals, and don't ask any more questions or I will be forced to hurt you.

I am writing this book as a guide for my followers. The pro-Christ, the boy Jesus, made a big mistake in not writing his ideas down himself, in so far as you could call them ideas. But then again, he didn't have my advantages. He was probably illiterate, whereas I have an excellent degree from a good university. Whatever the reason, his failure has led to thousands of people setting themselves up as interpreters of his Holy Word, from Peter to Aquinas to Jimmy Swaggart.

So that's the reason for this book. I'm laying down the law, saying what I want to say, and I'm saying it myself because I don't want to spawn generations of charlatans. I am, in consultation with a number of colleagues, formulating a series of Guidelines for the Implementation of Evil, and I intend to put them in this book so that they can be used as a source of reference by my followers both now and when my Reign of Terror has begun. The guidelines will be written unambiguously, will be reader-friendly, and will constitute a definitive guide to understanding the nature of Evil and how to put it into effect smoothly and efficiently.

I'm not writing it like his bible, by the way, with its begats and thou shalts. If the bible is a load of old tosh there's no point in emulating it. I'm writing in plain English, just as we always do at the Scottish Office, and observing the Cardinal Rule (not that cardinals observe it) Keep It Short — that way it's easier for the cretins who need your guidance to understand it. I'm having the Grocer put headings at the start of all the chapters, for ease of reference. I have also told him to write down whatever I say, using my exact words, and on no account to deviate from what I say in any way whatsoever. It is my feeling that the book will represent a major asset in the forthcoming Implementation of Evil process, and that it will provide my apostles, acolytes, followers and slaves with both comprehensive practical guidance and a theoretical grounding in the Nature and Conceptual Identity of Evil.

Guidelines on the Implementation of Evil – Underlying Principles I

1. There is no chaos so great, nor any so deep, that an attempt to organise matters will not make it worse.

2. The power of human beings to organise events is in inverse proportion to the importance of those events.

3. Administration is the key to the effective implementation of Evil.

MY NAME

I was christened Hector. Hector Hepton. My parents thought it euphonious, but it was not a kind thing to give that particular Christian name to a child in the early 1960s. My schooldays were made Hell by a puppet dog on television. Children tormented me by saying that I was a silly old Hector, and alleging that I was married to a cat and lived next door to a frog. If someone said this to me now I would shrivel them, or cast them into a Pit of Despair, without a second thought, and be none the worse for the experience, but at the time I was hurt by the allegations, false though they were. You feel these things deeply when you are young.

When I grew older, approaching my teenage years, and Hector's House was no longer on the television, people began to call me Heck. I didn't mind this at all. It went very well with the image I was trying to put across.

But then they found out about my middle name. My earthly father, the husband of my mother, was the Latin master at one of the town's better schools. He didn't really need to work, having a private income, so he taught Latin. He called me Sextus, after some Roman, and because I was born on the 6th June. It came out at the start of term one year. The English master read out all our names – he took a great delight in this kind of humiliation – and my torment started all over again. For the rest of my time at school – the next seven years – I was called Sexy Hexy. Again, there was a time in my life when I would have positively welcomed such an appellation, but at the time I resented it, sullenly and spitefully.

Perhaps, though, this too was part of my Destiny. The name-calling did at least inure me to the barbs of my peers. Perhaps my father, in his finite and earthly wisdom, was motivated by a deeper force than he could understand. Maybe, on the other hand, in this as in all else, he was just an insignificant speck in My History. He was a source of sperm, and nothing else.

I thought about changing my name when my parents died, but I was only 14 and I wouldn't have known what to change it to. Nigel, perhaps.

A COSMOLOGICAL ARGUMENT

Some of my wilder followers, my wayward Children, have tried to divine from my name evidence of my True Nature. We need, they argue, material evidence with which to convert the unbeliever. I have my doubts about this. I do not care about the unbelievers. They are damned, they are doomed. Why bother trying to convert them? Besides, I'm not at all sure that I want to start a religion. I just want to get on with the Reign of Terror.

Anyway, my own feelings don't seem to stop my followers, some of them anyway, from engaging in this kind of conjecture. There is, they say, a beautiful symmetry in the way all the aspects of my earthly being point to my Evilness. My name, they say, is the Mark of the Beast. Hector is shortened to Hexy, and Hex is a six – there are six sides in a hexagon. Sextus means six or, strictly, sixth.

This is, however, specious in the extreme. For one thing, if you carry the analysis forward into my surname, you find that if Hector and Sextus are sixes, then Hepton is a seven (like a heptagon), which means that if my name is the Mark of the Beast then we have been previously misinformed and the Mark of the beast shall be 667. It's close, I admit, but it's not convincing.

This does not stop them from constructing the argument, though. John the Divine got it slightly wrong, they say. He said 667, but it got mistranslated, they say. Pish and tosh, I reply. I will put a stop to such speciousness. Just do what I tell you to do, I say, and stop trying to justify it. That is a form of Faithlessness which will get you damned.

There are similar arguments about my birth date – the 6th of the 6th, 1965. But even discounting the fact there is a one, a nine and a five in there as well as three sixes, to choose that third six from four figures seems to me to be selective to the point of arbitrariness, though what they say is that it is the decade that is important – we always talk about the fifties, the sixties, the seventies and so on. In which case, the Mark of the Beast shall be 6665. Twaddle, of course, but that's religious types for you.

Besides, I refuse to justify myself. If people want to believe in me, and many do, their belief must stand or fall by faith alone.

The Grocer of Doom here, he believes in me, but he is too stupid to construct an argument. He is a tormented turnip. He believes everything I tell him. He is a worthless sack of poop and dung.

Yes, write that down. Poop has two Os.

Guidelines on the Implementation of Evil – Underlying principles II

1. Chaos is the Mother of Evil. Where Chaos is established, Evil shall surely follow.

2. We must, therefore, strive to cause Chaos, and to perpetuate her.

3. After Chaos has been established for a significant period of time, we will begin our Administration.

4. It is estimated that this will take between six and eight months.

VENGEANCE MAY BE SWEET, BUT IT IS NOT FOR ME

I want here to point out that I am not in this for personal revenge. My concerns are on a cosmic scale, and far surpass the personal. I have suffered, it is true, but I don't care. I am doing this because it is my Destiny, because it has to be done, because what will be will be. Que sera, sera.

That is not to say that there are not individuals who, when the Great Day comes and my Reign on Earth begins, won't be singled out for special treatment.

Mr Armstrong, who taught me in the third year of primary school and beat me in front of the whole school, will be shrivelled.

Graham Murray, Paul Hunter, Craig Chalmers, Gerry Malone and Martin Forsyth, who bullied me when I was on my way home from my trumpet lessons, will have their limbs and testicles torn from their bodies, and will be roasted over an eternal fire.

Mrs McGibbon, who reported me to the police when I was twelve for pushing down her garden wall and setting fire to her garden shed, will be dragged from her grave, re-animated and forced to watch herself decompose.

Alan Urquhart, who got me arrested by telling tales on me to a dairy farmer and the police, and who thwarted my chosen career, will be melted and left to fry in his own dripping.

My father and mother will be locked in a room with each other for all eternity.

MY GLITTERING CAREER COMMENCES

When I left school I went to St Andrews University to study Divinity. It was a bit of a wrench leaving Edinburgh, being so far from the centre of things, from civilisation, but I came back at weekends. Besides, I knew a lot of people in my year from school.

I was thinking of becoming a minister of the Church of Scotland. This now seems like the natural career choice for the proto-antichrist, though my motives for wanting to become a minister were not at all clear to me at the time. I had always had, I thought, some sort of religious leaning. Of course, when I was a child I had no idea of my True Nature, but I was aware of some spiritual dimension to my being, so I thought I was a Christian. You do rather tend to assume these things. Especially in Scotland. Especially in Edinburgh. Especially if you're of the right sort.

I didn't really believe, of course, not in the substance

of what I was being told. Not in all that God rubbish and Jesus stuff, but, I thought I did at the time. I was most enthusiastic about going to church every Sunday, at least for a few years, and I read my bible assiduously.

I suppose I wanted comfort. Mine had not been a happy childhood. I had had a number of unfortunate experiences.

Anyway, it was as a consequence of this that I had wanted to go into the ministry.

No there's no more. That's the end of this bit.

Because I don't feel I need to say any more at this point, that's why. Do not ask me any more questions or I shall destroy you. Now, let's do some more guidelines.

Guidelines on the Implementation of Evil – Underlying principles III

1. Bureaucracy

2. Many think of Armageddon, our ultimate goal, as involving total disorder. Complete anarchy

3. They are right. But bureaucracy – wild, rampant bureaucracy, completely unfettered – is an aspect of this few have ever considered.

4. For it is both a symptom, and a cause, of disorder, and people's inability to cope with it. They see a disordered Universe, they try to impose order on it, they make it worse.

5. Bureaucracy is my friend.

6. That would make a good marketing slogan in the USA.

7. 'And behind the Four Horsemen there shall walk a man in a raiment of grey with a faint self-coloured pin-stripe, and he shall be called Mr Hepton from Administrative Services.'

A DOOR IS CLOSED

My plans to join the ministry were thwarted whilst I was in my second year at University. I had become involved with a secret society called the Cattle Killers – an unimaginative name, perhaps, but accurate. It was a convocation of people from many walks of life, but centred on the university, drawn together by their shared interest in bovine murder. I remained on the peripheries of the organisation, but, even so, I found the range and inventiveness of its activities quite impressive at the time.

They would push cows off cliffs, shoot them with guns, shoot them with bows and arrows, slit their throats, cut their hooves off and leave them to bleed, poison their feed, hire light aircraft and drop bricks on them, hit them with hammers, nail them to fences, chain their legs together and throw them in lochs, cut them in half with chainsaws (once lengthwise), soak them with fuel and set fire to them, sew their mouths up, set them in concrete, roll them down hills, put them on specially-adapted roller skates and tow them along the motorway until escape velocity was achieved, disembowel them with Japanese swords, smash them with axes, drive lorries into them, bury them up to the neck, put dynamite up their back passages, suffocate them with plastic bags. Then they would mutilate the corpses. Some members of the society would shag them. After every kill they would rip off the udders and wear them as hats, performing the Dance of the Psychotic Cockerel. They were particularly keen on the horned varieties of cattle as the horns were highly prized, and accorded their owners great status at gatherings of the society where they would be worn as both headgear and decorative phalluses.

The disadvantage of belonging to such an organisation, though, is the risk it brings with it of exposure to Society's petty, frightened moralising. I do not want to go into the details here – beyond saying that it involved the deliberate treachery of the organisation's honorary president, Alan Urquhart – but I had the misfortune of being caught in a compromising position with an expiring cow, and was arrested. Charges were pressed, and I was due to appear in court.

The university authorities managed to hush it up, however, for fear of the scandal my trial would cause. For the same reason I avoided being expelled. I was allowed to finish my degree, but it was made plain to me in a very sticky interview with the Dean of Faculty that I would never be allowed to join the ministry. He assured me that he, personally, would go to great lengths to prevent me from becoming a minister. He would put the word out that I was a 'bad sort', as he put it. He would tell his colleagues. He would tell his old students. He had a great deal of influence, he said.

He became quite agitated in the course of the interview. Actually went red in the face. This was the first time anyone had told me I was the Antichrist. I shrugged it off, put it down to the fact that the old fool was a bit peeved. I was more concerned about the enforced change to my career plans.

It seemed, at the time, like a major disappointment. Now I see it as Destiny.

BUT ANOTHER ONE OPENS

My disappointment did not last that long, as I soon discovered my gift for administration. I had always been organised. As a child I had always filed my toys first by category and then alphabetically within the categories (Dinky cars, for instance, were filed under V for Vehicles; subclass: cars; in shoeboxes 3 and 4 of the shoeboxes marked 'd'). The bookshelves in my bedroom were organised according to a system of my own devising which was an improvement on the Dewey Decimal. But my gift didn't really come into its own until I was twenty or so. I had been made Treasurer of the Theology Society, and Secretary of the University Liberal Club. I discovered that I was very good at ordering their affairs.

I straightened up the Theology Society's financial procedures, and completely re-organised its record keeping. I improved the internal administration of the Liberal Club so radically that one of my tutors (a club member) suggested that I consider a career in public sector administration, where my talents would be used to great effect. He, as it happened, had a nephew who had a position of some responsibility in the Scottish Office Education Department, and he would have a word to see what could be done.

MY NAMES

i. I have been thinking about what I said about my given names. It is strange how, sometimes, our names change as we become who we were really meant to be.

ii. I have many names, but the real ones I only found out after I had been Revealed. It is the same for all of us who follow the Path of Evil.

iii. Some call me The Beast, others The Evil One. Some call me the Prince of Darkness and others the Lord of the Flies, but I abjure these aristocratic pretensions and will not answer.

iv. My names are legion. Sometimes I sign myself R McGeddon. It is a joke.

v. I am He Who Lurks in the Shadow, He Who Watches, The Darkness In Your Soul, Your Worst Nightmare, Reckoning, Judgement, The Destroyer, The Enemy, Chaos, The Shriveller, The One with the Forked Prong, the Impaler, The Rogerer, Black Destiny, The Devil's Spawn, Spawn of Satan, the Bringer of Dark Light, The End of the World. I do not mind what name I am called.

vi. Please don't call me Hector.

ON INFALLIBILITY

I am not infallible. Unlike His Holiness the Dope. When you are the Embodiment of Evil, you do not have to be. If you get things wrong they can turn out worse than they would have done had you got them right, and that is good, if you see what I mean.

Much of my life has been ruled by Destiny, but I have made mistakes. I chose the Grocer as a slave, but he is not worthy of so exalted a position.

I made another mistake just after I had taken up my junior administrative position on leaving university.

I had realised that the career which lay ahead of me was not going to be glamorous, and I was, of course, unaware, at this point, of my True Nature. I wanted to try something with more excitement than administration would afford, so I tried my hand at stand-up comedy.

Many of the people I had known over the years had told me that I was witty, a born comedian, had I ever thought of going professional. With that quickfire wit of yours you're bound to be a success, they said. You'll be great with hecklers. Many of our greatest comedians are lugubrious, gloomy buggers like yourself, they said. On the strength of this, I got myself a floor spot at a comedy venue in Edinburgh. I billed myself as Hector Hepton the High Priest of Humour.

It was not an unqualified success.

Quite the reverse. It was the one time I have known in my adult life what it is to be humiliated.

Part of the problem lay in the fact that I had not realised that the key to comedy is having some jokes written beforehand. It is no good going on stage and thinking of something witty to say, because it doesn't work. Especially the first time.

My audience, I must say, was particularly savage. It received me in stony silence, then started screaming obscenities and hurling coins, bottles, and at least one piece of fruit at me. I was quite startled at its ferocity and intolerance.

It is probable, of course, that Destiny did not want me to go down that path, and had prompted the most vicious of comedy fans to go out that night. Destiny wanted me back on the path she had marked out for me, and I obeyed. I resigned myself to a humdrum life, not knowing what lay in store for me. It was the last time I ever tried to make my own way.

As it was, it took me weeks to recover from the hurt and the humiliation. I buried my face in the folds of my wife's dress, though we were not married at this point, and let her make it better for me. She was very good at that.

The episode also taught me that a boring job is not necessarily a bad thing. If it isn't glamorous sitting there all day writing memos, filing pieces of paper, drafting reports and answering the telephone, at least it isn't very risky.

Guidelines for the Implementation of Evil

The advantages of Evil

1. There is a dimension to existence of which people who merely exist are unaware.

2. To experience this dimension you must give yourself up completely. Give yourself up to Evil.

3. It is also possible to experience it by giving yourself up to good.

4. But this is harder. And less rewarding.

A CAREER IN ADMINISTRATION

I don't want to say much about it really.

I joined up when I left University. I joined the Scottish Office Education Department as a Senior Administrative Officer. I did well, even though it was very boring. I was soon promoted to Executive Officer, then to Higher Executive Officer, then to Senior Executive Officer. I started doing really well when I was transferred out of Education and into the internal bureaucracy of the Scottish Office. I did so well that I was promoted many times, until I reached extremely lofty heights. Head of Administrative Services. I have particular responsibility, at the moment, for ordering the affairs of the Scottish Parliament, ensuring that its business runs smoothly, that support mechanisms are in place, that the resources allocated to it are not misappropriated. Indeed, I was responsible for a great deal of the organisation which made the establishment of the parliament possible in the first place. I was the ideal man for the job. I'm very well connected, you know, and I've always felt that Scotland deserved a parliament of its own and some voice in the running of its own affairs. One magazine article – only a business magazine, but still, a magazine – named me last year as one of the fifty most powerful men in Scotland. They said I was an 'unseen mover wielding enormous influence, a backroom wheeler-dealer who, having overcome personal tragedy last year, now controls a massive budget and one of the most important government departments in Scotland.' Little do they know.

Why should I say more? This is not my life story, it is

a book of Evil. It tells my followers what they should be doing and what they should be thinking. I shall only tell them things which have some bearing on that. Just write and shut the heck up.

OTHER REVELATIONS

I suppose I should tell you about the three times I was told I was the antichrist before I went to that party and was Revealed to Myself in All My Glory. It will be useful background information if nothing else.

The first, as I've already said, was the Dean of Divinity at university. I had never liked him. I thought him a silly, old, stuffy numpty, but then he was a dean and being a silly, old, stuffy numpty is a dean's job. I was summoned to see him shortly after the police had let me go pending a court appearance after they arrested me for the cow thing.

The Dean told me I was a very disreputable young man. It had come to light in the course of the cow thing that I had a previous record of criminal activity, some of it involving cruelty to animals, even though it was all pretty petty stuff and I'm not at all sure that pigeons even count as animals. He told me I was wicked and got himself really worked up. He told me I was more suited to devil worship than to the ministry of Christ.

Then he told me I was the Antichrist. It just sort of slipped out. Like a bolt from the blue. I looked at him askance. Even he looked a bit surprised at what he'd said, as if he hadn't known what he was saying.

He calmed down a bit after that, and said I could finish

my degree and that, despite his misgivings, he would do his best to persuade the police to drop the charges against me, but that I could forget the ministry. Then he ordered me out of his sight, and expressed the desire never to have to see me again. One of these days I shall pay him a return visit.

HIGH STREET STORY

This isn't a revelation, just a story. One day, shortly after my interview with the Dean, as I was walking down the High Street in Edinburgh a man dressed in black came up to me and said:

'I am at your bidding, O Master. Do with me what you will.'

I replied, 'What?'

So he repeated himself. 'I am at your bidding O Master. Do with me what you will.'

I told him that I still didn't understand what he was trying to say, and he said:

'Oh. Sorry. My mistake,' and walked off.

As I say, I don't count this as a Revelation because I didn't have a clue what he was talking about. I put it in here to show you that my True Nature must have been apparent to others long before it was known to me. Even the Dean had seen it in his silly, stuffy old numptyish way.

I have, by the way, met the Man in Black since. He's very nice. Very cruel. You'd probably think he was quite mad. I expect that we'll find him quite significant later on.

One day I may ask him to hurt you, badly. Then again, I may not. I might well do it myself.

REVELATION II

Revelation number two. Yes write it out in full if you like. I don't care. Look, it makes no difference to me whatsoever how you write it, as long as people can understand. Use the number or write it out.

If you don't get on with it now I will write it myself in your blood. I will flay you and stretch out your skin and make you write it on that. Shut up and write.

Revelation no 2 occurred at the seaside. I was drunk, out with a bunch of divinity students for a day of debauchery at the beach. I had nearly been thrown out of the university and they were trying to cheer me up. It was good being the centre of attention for once.

We saw a fortune-teller's booth. It bore a sign saying Madame Lara, Who Knows the Secrets of the Mysterious Orient, Prophecies and Predictions. Fortunes Told, Palms Read. Tarot. Genuine Crystal Ball. My friends started egging me on. Go on, they said, have your fortune told, see what lies in store for you. They wanted to know how serious a blow to my future had been dealt to me.

I was reluctant, but they enticed me with promises of free drink for the rest of the day if I succumbed. I yielded.

I entered. The place looked like what I imagined a tart's boudoir would be. I did not know for sure as I had, at that point, never been in a tart's boudoir, though I had been in the National Gallery of Scotland, which I had been told was pretty much the same thing. Anyway, it was red, and there was a tasselled shade on the lamp.

Madame Lara, Who Knows the Secrets of the Mysterious Orient, invited me to sit down across the table from her. She asked me what method of prediction I would like her to use, so I told her that she probably knew the answer to this question already so let's not waste any more time. She said that she could tell the moment I walked in I was going to make some wisecrack, and that I had to take the interview seriously if her predictive powers were to work properly.

Then she said all right, as a token of my powers, I shall choose for you. I shall choose the method you would have chosen. I shall choose the Tarot.

As the Tarot was, indeed, what I had been going to say anyway, I was momentarily taken aback, but then I reasoned that it was probably by far the most popular method of fortune telling, that anyone who played cards as much as I did (and I was a student after all) would naturally plumped for the tarot and that she could probably tell from my appearance and physical type that this was likely to be the case.

She offered me a pack and asked me to shuffle it, take ten cards. I was then to hand them to her, one by one.

I have to tell you that I was very sceptical throughout this interview. I had never believed in fortune telling in general, and I couldn't see in particular why or how Knowing the Secrets of the Mysterious Orient would make it any more likely that you would be able to predict the course of events, so I was suspicious when Madam Lara began, as I saw it at the time, to feign horror at what she was seeing in the cards. It was, I thought, more than likely that she had been put up to this by my friends. This was just the sort of trick a bunch of divinity students would pull.

At first Madam Lara said, 'Oh dear, this looks black. Very dark'. I supposed that this was at least novel. I had been expecting her to say that I would meet a nice girl and have three children, all girls, that I would be healthy and do well in my job though I might not find true fulfilment on a personal level. Because of the novelty of what she was telling me, I decided to stick with the interview even though I still suspected a put-up job.

Then, as Madam Lara turned over the last card she screamed, 'No No No No No! Get Out Get Out Get Out! Get Away from me!' I asked her why, because I thought that I might as well play along with the charade, but all she said was, 'Go Away, go away and never come back.'

I was getting a bit tired of it now, so I asked why once more, a hint of anger, I imagine, in my voice, and she said, 'Can you not know?' She wrote something on a piece of paper and handed it to me saying, 'Take this. Now, please, I beg you, leave, leave immediately,' and she ushered me out into the street.

When I got outside I was smiling, because I was still sure that my friends had put her up to this, and expected them to burst into laughter. They, however, were all agog to know what had happened, or were very convincing if they were pretending to be, so I began to have my doubts.

I told them what had happened, looked at the piece of paper Madam Lara had given me and showed it to them. It had numbers on it – either 666 or 999, depending on which way up you were holding it. Perhaps, I said, she was threatening to call the police on me. Perhaps, one of my friends said, she's been having a word with the Dean and she was telling you you were the Antichrist. This got a big laugh. I shrugged it off.

Intriguingly, a few minutes later we saw an ambulance outside Madam Lara's establishment. One of the crew told us that she'd had a heart attack and died.

AND THEN . . .

After that, I don't remember anyone telling me I was the Antichrist for about four years.

Guidelines for the Implementation of Evil – Post-chaotic Procedures I

There is, as must be immediately apparent to all practitioners of Evil, more to Evil than Chaos alone. It follows, therefore, that other elements need to be introduced.

The implementation process will be greatly facilitated by the introduction of a number of contributory factors. These include:

- the establishment of universal egoism as a behavioural norm
- the denial of absolute moral precepts
- the introduction of non-rational modes of thought and, more importantly, discourse
- the encouragement of negative public emotional modality

Chaos, as has already been mentioned, is a necessary condition for the implementation of Evil, but is not sufficient i.e. you need to establish chaos first, but there are then other things which need to be done. The four conditions named above, in conjunction with a pre-established condition of chaos, would in most circumstances be sufficient to bring about the establishment of Evil, though these four conditions are not themselves necessary conditions. It is, in other words, entirely conceivable that there might be other conditions which, in a post-chaotic situation, might also lead to the establishment of Evil. However, the four above-named conditions are those which are considered those most likely to facilitate a smooth and successful implementation process. The subsequent sections of these guidelines will deal with each of the four conditions in turn.

REVELATION III

The third person to tell me I was the Antichrist was my wife. We had, at this point, been married for a couple of years.

We were lying in bed one night, and she said, 'You know, there is something very odd about you.'

I was offended, and asked her what she meant. We have, I said to her, known each other for more than ten years, and now you suddenly decide there is something very odd about me.

She said that she had always thought there was something odd about me, but she had never mentioned it before. It wasn't just the way I dressed or behaved. These were, she said, very odd, but she had been aware of them from the moment we first went out together at university, perhaps even when we'd danced together at one of those staged events where Academy boys and St George's girls exercise their fumbling, incompetent social skills. What she was talking about was something more fundamental. It was as if, she said, I was not quite human. She said that she sometimes used to look at me and wonder whether I was an alien, a being from another planet sent here to observe the human race and report back prior to an invasion.

I found this disturbing. I grew angry at her and told her to explain what she meant. She went on to say that she had begun to discern in me a capacity for total and infinite evil. There was, she said, something about the way in which I related to other people and our cats. It was, she said, as if I was not, after all, an alien, but was some kind of demon or creature from Hell. No, she said, more than that, perhaps I was the Antichrist. It was alright, though, she said, she didn't mind. She still loved me.

So, I thought, that's all right then. I'll forget all about it.

Guidelines for the Implementation of Evil – Post-chaotic Procedures II

The establishment of universal egoism as a behavioural norm

1. It is a simple precept that, if every person's principal objective is the satisfaction of his or her own wants and desires, the majority of people will fail to achieve their objectives and will, as a result, experience disappointment and frustration.

2. Furthermore, there will be a great deal of resentment of those who do achieve their goals.

3. From our point of view, this is a desirable state of affairs.

4. It is, to a certain extent, probable that the establishment of universal egoism will come about as a result of the establishment of chaos. However, this will by no means be a forgone conclusion.

5. However, there are, in contemporary western society, a number of pre-existing social and cultural conditions which will predispose any state of chaos, once established, to lead to the establishment of universal egoism as a behavioural norm. Principal amongst these is the fact that the dominant political ethos and practice of the late 20th century has been based on a set of individualistic-monetarist values which are sufficient for the establishment of universal egoism as a behavioural norm given the pre-establishment of chaos.

This is shite. Total and utter shite. I didn't understand that last bit at all. I haven't got a clue what he's ranting on about.

He never reads this shite, you know. He just spouts it all out and tells me to write it down. It's a load of old bollocks.

REVELATION

It was only after the fourth time I'd been told who I really was, Who I really was, (yes, yes, yes. Bastard) that all of this made sense. I suddenly realised that my Father – my True Father, not that pathetic and insignificant fool who lived with my mother – had been trying to tell me who

I was, Who I was, for years. Immediately things began to make sense to me.

You see, I'd always known I was a bit different. For one thing there was the Voice. I now recognised this as my Father's Voice, but it had been shouting inside my head for a long time. There were other things too. Streetlights always used to go out when I passed under them. I had a habit of breaking drinks-vending machines simply by pressing the Coffee White One Sugar button. I sometimes used to interfere with TV reception, and computers would crash when I tried to operate them. I once rendered the entire British Rail ticketing system a bubbling, slimy mess by asking for a return ticket to Gourock.

I had not, until I was Revealed to myself, thought of any of this as manifestations of supernatural power on my part. I had merely dismissed them all as one (or, indeed, many) of those things which just happen, but now I can see that they were all inevitable consequences of my being the Embodiment of Evil.

ALSO

Also, people used to stare at me in the street. They looked at me as if they recognised me, like they do when they see someone who has been on television. But it was not my face which they were recognising. What they were seeing in me was something much deeper, something which was also deep within themselves. Something Wicked.

AND ANOTHER THING

Something else which makes sense to me now that I can see it in context – dogs. They were always afraid of me. They used to back up, snarling, whenever I approached.

Also, milk. Used to turn sour. Some people can leave a carton of semi-skimmed in their fridges for days on end and it will still be drinkable. With me it would last a couple of hours and go rancid. I always had to go out in the morning to find something to pour over my cornflakes. This used to puzzle me. Even called in an electrician to look at the fridge. He sucked his breath in through his teeth, shook his head and said, 'nothing wrong with her, pal, as far as I can see'.

And my halitosis. I tried everything I could think of to get rid of it: constant tooth-cleaning, mouth washing, avoiding spicy foods. Nothing worked. My breath was foul.

It's not so sweet now, pal.

TIME TO MAKE MY MARK

That's what I decided when I had been Revealed to Myself. It was time to go out into the world and start doing things. Begin my Ministry. I was 32. It's around about the traditional age for making such decisions. I had, as I have said, lived as full and pleasant a conventional life as I believe it is possible to live, but I felt I had not done anything. Now I knew why.

Perhaps Ministry is the wrong word. I am not trying to start a religion here. I have no time for religious impulses. I had them when I was younger. They are pointless.

I do not want to preach to you. I want to show you the most effective ways of achieving real Evil. I myself shall be overseeing the implementation process, maintaining a strategic overview, and taking operational control of the more important initiatives, but I hope, as time goes by and I grow stronger in my power, to be able to delegate more and more responsibility for this aspect of my activities to my officers and operatives. The supernatural stuff, what you might call 'the gobbledegook', the walking on water and turning it into poison, is a useful tool, maybe, but it's not an integral part of the process. Effective organisation is the key. My career on this Earth is not so much a ministry as an Administry.

I began to formulate a plan. I knew that what I had to do was bring about a Reign of Terror on the Earth, but how to do it, that was the question. Guidelines would help, but there aren't any, which is why I'm having to write my own based on my instinctive understanding of Evil — it is, it seems to me, essentially a matter of organisation and motive. All my great role models have been in government (Hitler, Stalin, Pol Pot etc), though I am coming to admire the chief executives of some of the American multinationals and the Halifax Building Society. What I'm not sure of is precisely *how* to put this into practice. I am sure that I'm perfectly placed to do it. All my role models started out with a power base, and the fact that Edinburgh has a parliament all of its own now, and the fact that I'm looking after certain important aspects of the running of it, means that I have a real headstart. The question is simply what to do next. I have no doubt that I'll get there in the end, and I suppose that when I do I personally will have no more need for this book, though it may be a handy guide for my lieutenants. The writing of it is, in itself, something of a learning exercise.

I decided early on that the first thing to do was to overthrow everything, destroy people's way of life, create Chaos and Havoc. This would give Evil room to breed and grow. It seemed like too big a job for one man, albeit a man who was the very Embodiment of Evil, possessed of untold and, as yet, largely unexplored, powers. In any case, as I've already said, Evil – even the creation of Chaos and Havoc – is largely a matter of organisation, system, authority, and this implies not being able to do it on your own. It seemed to me, therefore, that I should go out and gather unto myself some Apostles.

My first was the Grocer.

It was a mistake. He is too worthless a snivelling piece of dung-caked slime to be an apostle. Nevertheless, he has his uses. I shall enumerate them later on. Perhaps.

THE GROCER OF DOOM

Oh, go on, then.

You'll like this bit, your moment of glory. I'll make it as unpleasant for you as I possibly can. I'll enjoy watching you write it down.

He was surrounded by fruit and veg, and was as malevolent a human being as I have ever encountered, but was too petty and lacking in imagination to be really evil.

The first thing you noticed about him in his shop was that he was too mean to use paper bags that were big enough to put all your carrots or whatever in. He would cram a pound of whatever vegetable you wanted into a paper bag the size of a ladies pocket handkerchief, and they would all fall out as soon as you left the shop. He had fly papers hanging from his ceiling, but they were old and covered in flies that looked as if they had been there since the beetles. I wonder how you've spelled that. Tell me.

No, that's wrong. B.E.A.T.L.E.S. Beatles.

It's a kind of joke.

Insects, yes, but the point is that there was a popular music ensemble in the 1960s, before your testicles had withered and your wallet had slammed shut for good, called the Beatles. You must have heard of them. Just shut up and write you ignorant little speck of a man. This is your moment of glory, posterity's record of your life's finest moment.

Ready?

To resume then.

But he wasn't just mean, he was full of spite. He used to spend hours and hours rubbing his own excrement onto dates. It took a long time because he had to unwrap each box carefully, take each date out, rub his filth onto it, put it back in the box, repeat this for every date in the box, and finally re-wrap the box so that you couldn't tell it had been tampered with. The only reason he can advance for having done this, (and I estimate that it used to take him a good 3 hours a day, allowing for the initial collection of the excrement) was that it was something to do, wasn't it? Nobody ever finds out, he said, because dates 'taste a bit like shit anyway'. He told me all grocers did it, that it was one of the secrets of the trade, but I took this to be a lie. Mind you, I met a food scientist once who told me that everybody looks for faecal undertones in food – it's one of the aspects of taste and smell we find appealing. I like that idea, the fact that even when we eat we are wallowing in filth and decay. I doubt that anything as considered as this was going through the Grocer's mind, however. In so far as he has a mind, it is just full of resentment and malice. There is no reflection there at all.

On the day I decided to recruit him I walked into his shop. He was selling beetroot to an old lady. I saw his eyes light up slightly, the merest flicker of excitement as her hand passed over the dates and hovered for an instant, and fade again as she changed her mind. When she had gone I stared at him. He shifted about, uneasily.

I was drawn to him, rather as, as a human child, I had been fascinated by insects. I used to watch them for minutes on end before squashing them. I understood him completely within seconds: it was all written there on his face and in the way he carried himself, in his expression of resentment and his furtive little actions. He had a sullen, spiteful moustache. I could see how he despised the little people who came into his shop for a packet of cooked beetroot and three small oranges. I knew that he would keep them waiting for five minutes longer than was strictly necessary, annoying them with his tuneless, grating whistle and his pointless own-up-baldie hairstyle. I knew what he was doing beneath his maroon drip-dry nylon grocer's overall.

I stared at him more.

We remained in these positions for 15 minutes. He said

nothing. He saw my total comprehension of him in my gaze, and he withered in it. 'You,' I said finally, 'are a worthless piece of dung.'

I turned on my heel and left.

I came back the next day and repeated the scenario. 'You,' I said, 'are a worthless piece of dung.'

On the third day of this he still raised no objection. After I had told him he was a worthless piece of dung, he spoke, but all he said was, 'who are you?'

I told him.

Then I told him that I needed a servant, and that in my service he could find some purpose, some sense of worth. I told him he would be rewarded, that, with me, he could find riches and power, that he would rule over sections of the globe, that he would have slaves to do his bidding.

I lied.

Then I told him I knew about the dates. And the sweeties.

THE SWEETIES

I know I told you I wouldn't mention the sweeties, but I only said that so that I could watch your face when I mentioned them.

In his shop, apart from the fruit and veg, he also sold sweeties.

He sold sweeties as a means of attracting small boys into his shop. He ogled them. He gave them free sweeties to encourage them to come back, but he never acted on his impulses towards them.

This was not out of conscience. He knows he is a vile, loathsome creature. He knows his impulses are repulsive, but makes no effort to change them.

It is weakness of will. He lacks the ability to carry his desires through to execution. He is as flaccid in spirit as he is in body.

NEVERTHELESS...

He has his uses. He can write quickly and legibly with a biro, and his spelling is competent.

Also, he is the source of a cheap and plentiful supply of fresh fruit and vegetables.

SECOND LIEUTENANT

I quickly realised that I was going to need apostles with more spunk in them.

One of the ones I chose was a girl, sorry, that sounded rather sexist. A young woman who worked in my organisation. We used to meet for sex in the toilets outside her office at 1pm on Tuesdays and Thursdays – the ladies on Tuesday and the men's on Thursday. I had, I remember, the devil of a time persuading her to take it in the mouth.

Once, whilst lurking in the car-park as I was wont to do in the afternoons, I caught her twisting the testicles of a junior colleague (called Malcolm something or other, I think). She was clearly enjoying herself.

He had, it transpired, caught her loading computer equipment into her car and accused her of stealing it. She had responded with a savagery that surprised him, and made him wish he had kept quiet. I watched the display for several minutes. She hurt him, then she hurt him more and said, 'If you whisper one word of this to anyone, something much, much worse will happen to you. Do you understand?'

He did. You could tell. She didn't really have to put it into words. There was something about her manner.

He assured her he would keep quiet. She told him that rather more was required than mere quietness. He would have to help her in future thefts, that was the only way she could be entirely sure of being able to trust him. He nodded and limped off, crying.

I was most impressed.

She didn't, I think, see me, though there has always been the idea hovering somewhere in the back of my head that this was perhaps a show she had put on for my benefit. It is the sort of thing she would be quite likely to do, and people with a desire to get ahead in the Scottish Office often behave with a similar degree of ostentation in front of their superiors, though rarely with such a degree of malice. They tend, more usually, to confine their attention-seeking to the writing of pointless papers, the calling of purposeless meetings, and the working of superfluous extra hours. As I say, her behaviour could have been motivated by similar considerations but I think, on the whole, that it is probable that I genuinely observed her unseen.

A few weeks later, after relations between us had been firmly established, I told her I had seen everything and invited her out for dinner. We went to Martin's. Over a good feed and a few bottles of claret she told me that she had been embezzling and stealing for years, and had been doing so in my department ever since she joined. It was, she said, easy if you knew how and had the confidence (she called it 'brass neck'). I questioned her motives – did she need money.

No, she said. She had plenty of money – even a private income. She was a St George's girl. A couple of years younger than my wife. Daddy was a banker. She stole because she enjoyed it. She stole for kicks.

The first time we had spoken socially was a few weeks before the basement and testicles incident, by the photo-copiers on the third floor of the office. I had heard that she had been appointed, of course, some months before, and I suppose that, as her ultimate boss, I should have introduced myself earlier, but I didn't like to mix with the staff. It's not to my personal taste to do so, and, in any case, mingling with the hoi polloi is not encouraged at the highest levels. As soon as I saw her, though, I was strangely drawn to her, as to no other.

'Hello,' she said.

'Hello,' I replied. 'You're new here, aren't you?'

'Not really,' she said. 'It's just that we've never met, although I've noticed you.'

I must admit to having felt a stirring in my trousers. It was the way she said it.

She gave me her card and a smile from her upturned face. The card read 'Judith X Heriot, Senior Press Officer'.

'My name's Judith,' she explained.

'Judy?' I asked.

'Judith,' she said.

'Oh,' I said. 'And what about the X?'

'Xenobia,' she said.

'Must hate your parents for that,' I said.

'Yes,' she said.

'Me too,' I said. 'Mine called me Sextus'.

'That's bad,' she sympathised.

'Maybe not as bad as yours, though,' I replied. 'Look, do you fancy a shag?'

'All right,' she said. 'Let's go to the toilets.'

'Your place or mine?'

Guidelines for the Implementation of Evil – Post-chaotic Procedures III

The denial of absolute moral precepts

1. This element is straightforward, and closely related to Post-chaotic Procedures II – the establishment of universal egoism as a behavioural norm. Indeed the two elements are mutually corollorating.

2. The denial of absolute moral precepts, given the establishment of universal egoism as a behavioural norm, will liberate people, encouraging or allowing them to act in their own interests without the enfetterment implied by the existence of universal moral precepts.

3. Thus, if, for example, the absolute prohibition on killing is lifted, people will be free to kill according to their own wants and needs.

4. The result of this will be rapid degeneration into a state of near anarchy. This will suit our purposes admirably.

5. The mechanisms for bringing about the denial of absolute moral

precepts are erosive, and are both simple and already in place. They include the following measures:

* the promulgation and proliferation of counter-examples to absolute moral precepts in popular entertainment, literature and mass media

* the mutual reinforcement of the erosion process and the political values discussed in Post-chaotic Procedures II:5.

This will be reinforced by the inevitable moral degeneration resulting from decades of social decadence – the number of absolute moral precepts which have fallen into abeyance within the last forty years is substantial. These include prohibitions on e.g. adultery and the coveting of the goods and chattels of neighbours.

JUDITH AT WORK

As I have said, I had heard of Judith before the encounter by the photocopier. I was her ultimate boss, after all. My work rarely brought me into contact with the little people who work in the offices, writing things and filing and talking to each other on the telephone and whatever else it is they do, but because of the seniority of my position and my line-management responsibilities I did get to hear about more or less everything which went on in the organisation. This was especially true of certain sorts of thing, and the sorts of thing Judith became involved in definitely counted as certain sorts of thing.

She had, in fact, been the subject of various memos to

me from the personnel department. In the sense that I took no action as a result of reading them, you could say that I ignored them. Indeed, it was a guiding rule of mine always to ignore memos from the personnel department.

They did, however, make interesting reading.

They concerned the way she treated her staff. She bullied them, not to put too fine a point on it. I suppose that personnel expected me to do something about it, but I always think that management techniques are best left to the individual.

Sometimes, a carrot and stick approach to management can be a great motivator. Reward them for successes, punish them for failures and transgressions.

Judith did not believe in carrots.

Other senior officials in the organisation used to tell me that they thought her slightly unbalanced. One, Mr Stewart from Planning and Research, said that I should look her up because the word was that she wasn't averse to sleeping with senior management to oil the wheels of her career. All this tended to make me think that she was definitely very interesting.

Of course, what all the people talking about her had overlooked was one simple fact. She was evil. That is, she was predisposed towards evil. Individuals by themselves (though I exclude myself from this rule, naturally) cannot be evil. True evil, as I have already said, is a feature of large organisations.

The signs of Judith's nature were all there. There were, for instance, many instances of her punishing people on highly arbitrary grounds. She once re-structured her entire staff, throwing (I seem to remember) her 14 underlings into a state of confusion and nervous exhaustion. She even combined the posts of her two deputies into one. The sole purpose of the exercise, as far as I could tell, watching from above, was to torment her staff. Especially the deputies, whom she made compete for the one remaining job. She dragged it out for months. She teased them, she bullied them, she played with them as a cat does with a mouse. After half a year or more, she suddenly and brutally appointed an outsider. This sort of thing is par for the course in the public sector, but it is usually caused by incompetence rather than being motivated by malice.

There was an uproar. There were appeals to the senior officials in the organisation. They came to me.

I did nothing, of course. I was, by that time, coming to admire her tremendously.

INTRODUCTION TO EVIL

I told Judith who I was, look at me, look at me, Who I was, during the wiping off stage of one of our toilet encounters. She was wrapping 12 feet of tissue around her right hand (I produce a lot of seed – it is part of my Nature) and was about to start mopping, when I said to her 'I am Evil Incarnate'.

She told me I was a real tiger. 'No,' I said. 'I am Evil Incarnate. I am the Beast, the Destroyer of Souls etc. The Antichrist.'

'Oh,' she said, 'I knew there was something about you . . . I don't normally do this kind of thing, you know. It was just that I found you strangely compelling from the start. I always wondered why.'

'I would like you to be my Lieutenant,' I said. 'I would like you to be my Minister, the Administrator of Evil, my right hand. I would like you to Execute My Will.'

'OK then,' she replied.

'Good,' I said. 'See you next door on Thursday.'

REALLY?

All right, it took a bit longer than this. She looked askance at me for a good few minutes. She called me a tosser and told me not to be stupid. Maybe she thought I was mad. I don't know and, frankly, I don't care.

I convinced her eventually by outlining my plans for the future – development and implementation of Evil culminating in world domination – and telling her that I would need a close ally at the Scottish Office. I would be moving on to bigger and better things, of course, though Edinburgh would always be my power base – my house is here after all, and I saw no reason to forsake it. I would simply be occupied with bigger things. I would need someone to hold the reins at the centre, someone to control the parliament and all the machinery of government once Scotland had become independent (with my help) and a world power in its own right, once it had become the centre of my global operations. Someone who was in, or whom I could manoeuvre into, a position of great power and influence herself.

This was when she finally took the bait. An appeal to naked self-interest. You get the general idea.

Of course, I didn't really know exactly how I was going

to achieve world domination at that point, and I still don't, frankly, but I expect it will all come naturally to me at the appointed time. The important thing is to believe in yourself. This is what persuades others of the truth of what you're saying. This is what persuaded Judith.

Guidelines for the Implementation of Evil

Procedures

1. In Evil, as in all things, the correct procedures must be followed.

2. The correct procedures for the various stages of the implementation of Evil are set out in the companion volume to this guide: *Procedures for the Implementation of Evil*

3. In the event of any matter arising, and that matter not being covered in *Procedures for the Implementation of Evil*, the matter should be referred to a senior figure (myself, or one of the executive officers) for a decision.

4. Any deviation from the correct procedures will be viewed as, depending on the circumstances, either failure or betrayal. The consequences of both are extremely severe.

I found Meek, drunk and dejected, early one morning outside the outpatients clinic at the Royal Edinburgh Hospital. I had been there before and had noticed her – something about her caught my eye, and she seemed to have many of the qualities I was looking for. This day, though, I was completely sure that she was right for my purposes. She definitely had the qualities I was looking for – in abundance. She had just been spurned by yet another lover, and was lying at the bottom of the Pit of Despair. I took her under my Big Black Wing.

She was a psychiatric nurse – the Royal Ed is a psychiatric hospital. She spent her days ministering to drooling basket cases (and, she readily confesses, fleecing them for petty cash) and her nights sleeping with psychiatrists, clinical psychologists, occasional psychoanalysts, doctors, surgeons, registrars, and any others★ who she thought might be persuaded into marriage to provide her with a decent living and cater for her sophisticated tastes. There was, she said, little difference between the daytime and nocturnal activities – she could tell me things about doctors which would make my hair curl, or at the very least depress me.

Sooner or later, though, every one of the psychiatrists, psychologists, psychoanalysts, doctors and what have you threw her over, despite her obvious charms and enormous erotic potential. She had only become a nurse, she said,

★ She said later that, of all of her sleeping partners, she thought she preferred the psychiatrists as they were better hung up. She told me this was a nurse joke. I've heard worse.

in the hope of attaching herself to a wealthy doctor, and her failure to do so, in spite of giving her all, had made her bitter.

She became my Lieutenant. I started to recruit her that very day. I showed her my power, little by little, and revealed myself to her. It took me some months to convince her that I was who Who I said I was, but I was taking it slowly. I wanted to get it right.

I knew that she could be very useful to me. If she could get me access to some of her more influential patients, we would have made a fine start. I could restore them to a semblance of normality and send them out into the world to do my bidding. This is, after all, the classic procedure for starting your own religious-type organisation. I would have a small army of wealthy and powerful nutters at my command. I could wreak some serious havoc. I could set up a network of evil-doers.

As an inducement to her, to encourage her to be loyal, that very day I gave her a lure.

Yes. A lure.

A-L-L-U-R-E.

You idiot. You stupid, stupid, worm-eaten half-rotted turnip of a sad, stinking little man. Sex, not fishing. Allure. Sexual attractiveness of a magnetic kind. Power over, in this case, men. Or, at least, psychiatrists, psychologists, psychoanalysts etc. She would now be able to tease them, have them drooling and following her around. She spurns them. She drives them wild.

It was a simple matter of restoring her confidence (or rather increasing her confidence – it had never been great, otherwise she would never embarked on her husband-getting exercise in the first place). I showed her how to use her body. I showed her how to exude sensuality. It worked like a charm.

Guidelines for the Implementation of Evil – Post-chaotic Procedures IV

The encouragement of non-rational modes of thought and, more importantly, discourse.

An important factor to bear in mind is that Evil itself, being chaotic and disordered, is, essentially, non-rational. It might even be argued that it is irrational. I do not propose to explore this issue here. Let it be sufficient to say that, from the rational point of view, no-one in their right mind would willingly foster and encourage the development of Evil – to do so would run counter to the very nature of rationality.

A key step, therefore, in the implementation process, is the encouragement of non-rational modes of thought and, more importantly, discourse. Discourse is the more important of these two elements simply because it is non-private, and is a central part of the encouragement process. It is thought plus active communicativity, facilitating the spread of ideas (however irrational they may be). By encouraging people to think and, more importantly, talk in a manner which is contrary to the rational, we are therefore overcoming a major barrier to the implementation process.

There are a number of steps which can be taken to facilitate this process:

    * the encouragement of non-rational faddishness. This includes

belief in illogical thought-systems such as religions (though over-adherence to these brings its own problems), mysticism, existentialism and some forms of political philosophy. The widespread use of hallucinogenic drugs also facilitates the process.

* the spreading of a hatred of or lack of respect for rationality by encouraging people to put more emphasis on their emotions (despite the fact that the rationality/emotionality distinction is a false one – what matters is that it is perceived to be true). We are already well along the way towards the achievement of this goal.

* the enfosterment of anti-intellectual attitudes. These are already established within certain societies (in England, for instance, and to a lesser degree in Scotland).

LAWYER

Meek was as good as her word. Two days after her induction into the programme, she came to me with a prominent lawyer. He is a bastion of the legal establishment – you might even recognise his name – I know I did. He was at school with my father. But what you might not know is that he had been detained by the authorities after what was politely termed a 'breakdown' which had culminated in his throwing his television set into the docks at Leith.

The story put about by the authorities and the legal establishment was that he was suffering from stress and had taken a short holiday from his duties in order to recuperate, but Meek told me that what had actually happened was that he had developed the belief that the American lunatic science fiction writer and mystic L Ron Hubbard had been giving him messages, from beyond the grave, through the TV. The learned gentleman had found this most upsetting, not least because, being a betting man, he enjoyed the occasional flutter on the horses but had been unable to watch the race results because L Ron kept interrupting with messages.

The ironic thing about this was that the messages continued even after the set was submerged, though they were more bubbly than before. It had something to do, he believed, with the conducting properties of salt water, which had fused the connections in the TV set. In fact, he was in a worse situation than before as he could not now reach out and turn the thing off.

When Meek brought him to me he was a total mess. It was easy to calm him down, to talk to him, to win him round, to supplant and usurp Mr Hubbard in his consciousness. He gets his messages from me now.

He was my first lawyer. Not my last, though. Not by a long chalk.

He was also the first recruit to what has become, over the months and years, a substantial network of evil-doers. It is a network which reaches into every walk of life, which has its fingers in every pie, its eyes and ears in every room, its member in every orifice. It is my network, and it is powerful. Edinburgh is mine.

EDINBURGH IS MINE

It really isn't all that difficult to take control of a town like Edinburgh, even though it is the most magnificent place on the whole planet (this being one of the reasons my Father caused me to be born here). Although it has many inhabitants, it is actually run by a tiny clique of people who have certain characteristics in common. A degree of wealth, for instance. Many of them are nutters, for another. Almost all of the older ones were at school with my father. Their wives with my mother. The new generation were at school with me, their wives with my wife. Everyone knows everyone else. It's all very cosy and very nice and cliquey and, once you've started to exert your influence over a significant number of them, the town is yours. And because Edinburgh is the capital and controls the whole country, by controlling it you can control the whole country. Soon, Scotland will be its own nation again. My Father has foreseen it. The people of Scotland have always wanted it. I have always wanted it. This, my Native Land, will be my power base as I spread my tentacles out over the world. Caledonia will arise and be a nation again. It will be the New Israel, the New Rome, the black heart of my dark empire.

CHALK AND CHEESE

That's Judith and Meek. Chalk and cheese. Calcium and Camembert.

Think of the way I recruited them. Judith took me at my word when I said I was Evil Incarnate. It only took a few minutes to convince her. She is malicious herself, a person of great power, and she knows it, and she was able to look at me and recognise me for what I am. I like to think that she saw in me a kindred, if superior, spirit. I let her think of us as partners, as similar, even though she is mortal and I am the Embodiment of Evil. I got her interested by saying things to her. Things like, 'They're so small and insignificant, aren't they, the rest of humanity?' and she would agree. She once asked me why I persistently broke various petty rules and regulations, like the prohibition on smoking in the lifts. I said, 'Rules and regulations are for the little people. You know that.' She agreed. It was one of her fundamental principles.

More importantly, she also saw in me a way to advance her own interests. Her own interests, after all, are her main interest. I think it is probably true that she was interested in me at first because I was her boss, and because I was in a position of influence at work. But then she was interested in me because I was powerful in Evil, unless she was just going along with me to get on my good side, curry favour, manoeuvre herself into a strong position. But no. She has done such valuable work since then. She must believe. And she *is* powerful. She would have been powerful without me. I will have to watch her.

Meek is much more giving. I had to go to great lengths

to convince her I was Who I said I was. I had to show her something, give her something. I gave her her sexual power. To tell the truth, it was already there, as it is in so many women. I simply brought it out.

Then I brought out her total self-confidence. I did it by appealing to her mothering instincts, by pretending to be like the drooling basket cases she works with, despite my fine clothes and my private income and my handsome appearance. These were just the bait she needed. I hooked her with sympathy. I cried on her shoulder and let her comfort me. I let her dominate me. I told her a sad story about myself. Mentioned my wife and let her nurse me. She nursed me so much that she began to trust me, love me even, then I told her I was evil. By then it was too late. She was mine. Forever.

AND IF THEY WERE DOGS

Judith would be a fierce Doberman Pinscher, and Meek would be a faithful Border Collie.

The Grocer's an ancient asthmatic Chihuahua guarding a bank.

Guidelines for the Implementation of Evil – Post-chaotic Procedures V

The establishment of negative public emotional modality

This is the key to our success, and will therefore be discussed at greater length than the other conditions hereto enumerated.

Negative public emotional modality is the fertiliser with which we will prepare the ground for our Reign of Terror. Only when the emotional outlook of each and every person is entirely negative can Evil be fully implemented.

There are a number of pre-conditions which must be satisfied before the establishment of negative public emotional modality can be successfully achieved. Principally these include the encouragement of non-rational modes of thought and, more importantly, discourse (Post-chaotic Procedures IV), coupled with what practitioners of Evil refer to as bedarkenment (the opposite of enlightenment). What this means is the breaking down of the psychological barriers which people erect to keep themselves a) sane and b) happy.

Consider the following, which we hold to be true: Most people have ambitions and dreams. No people fully achieve these. Therefore, most people are sad and pathetic failures.

This would ordinarily be the case, but for the existence of the psychological barriers referred to above. These barriers take the following forms:

* house, home and family, and the comfort and security which these provide

* the prospect of life after death, which deflects attention from the qualitative paucity of earthly existence

* psychological defence mechanisms such as deferred fulfil-ment strategies in which the person maintains, apparently in all sincerity, that they simply have not achieved their aims and desires yet, but may do so next week, next month or, more commonly, next year.

The breaking down of these barriers will not necessarily be easy.

Since the mental health and happiness of many persons depends solely upon the existence and integrity of the barriers a great deal of resistance will be encountered. Nevertheless, the breaking down of the barriers is of the utmost importance.

One method of achieving barrier break-down is by argument, or pointing out to the populace at large that the barriers outlined above (and the several others which are employed) are hollow shams. Given, however, the amount of resistance which will inevitably be encountered, such a strategy is unlikely to succeed in any but a small minority of cases.

Another might be by political subversion – attacks upon the totems which sustain the barriers (law, church, nation-state, family etc). However, for the same reasons, this is likely only to appeal to a minority.

A third possibility is that the measures outlined in Post-chaotic Procedures IV – the encouragement of non-rational modes of thought and, more importantly, discourse – might in themselves lead people to negative emotional modality. This will be particularly true of e.g. those existentialists who realise that they are alone in a barren universe, leading meaningless, insignificant lives for a brief instant before they vanish into oblivion.

The one tactic which is most likely to succeed, however, is the establishment of Despair.

Our next recruit was a gallery owner. Smallish gallery in the New Town. You must know it. The proprietor's a prominent supporter of the Scottish National Party.

You may think that recruiting a gallery owner is a waste of time and I dare say that in any other city you'd be right, but people of his sort wield an enormous amount of influence in Edinburgh. Not because they went to the right school (though they did, of course, otherwise they wouldn't be running art galleries) but because the people who run the town all have their arty farty pretensions.

It has to do with Edinburgh being the most civilised city on Earth. This, at least, is the view in Edinburgh, and it is correct. This is why it must be destroyed. Edinburgh has art galleries and museums, castles and cathedrals, festivals, theatres, restaurants, palaces and god knows what else because it is the centre of the universe.

I met him at lunch, the gallery owner. At the Cafe St Honore off Thistle Street. Charming establishment. They do a fine lunch. Have you been, Grocer? Of course not. They don't serve turnips. It's very popular with persons of quality. The Edimbourgeoisie. I was in there with Mr Stewart from the office just the other day. Head of Planning and Research. He likes it in there too, and his father's a lord. My father taught him Latin, you know.

Guidelines for the Implementation of Evil

Despair

1. Make friends with Despair.

2. I lived with it a long time before my True Nature was revealed to me. It made me more willing to accept the truth about myself.

3. It will have the same effect on others. It was Despair that brought me Meek.

4. There is a lot of it about.

5. But there will be a great deal more.

IT'LL GET WORSE

Thinking about that last guideline, it suddenly struck me how brilliant it was of My Father to send me here to Scotland. Land of Despair, even if its people are perversely cheerful about it.

Think about their catchphrase. It'll get worse, you know. People say that to you all the time. About the weather and the railways, football and work. It could be hailing, freezing, one of those knife-edge north winds blowing and you'll say to someone 'terrible, isn't it?' and they'll say 'Aye. It'll get worse.' And it's always true.

I've rendered it into Latin. A tribute to my father, the

earthly one. Not that he deserved it. *Male est futurum.* I like the double meaning. It'll get worse. The future is evil. The future *is* Evil. My father would have approved. I think I shall adopt this officially as my motto. Put it on a coat of arms. Severed arms, perhaps. No don't write that down, it's just a little joke. I must have a word with the Lord Lyon next time I see him. I think I'm still on his Christmas card list.

CHUCKLE

It always made me chuckle, in the early days, the thought of sitting there in that office, pushing pieces of paper around, filing memos, issuing directives, drawing up procedures, administering the business of the new parliament, speaking to members of the cabinet, hobnobbing with the first minister (one of ours from the very early days – you can see the evil glint quite plainly, I'm surprised no-one has noticed it) to think that I was already some sort of a power in the land, but that I would soon be supreme.

My network was growing from deep within the Scottish Office, expanding into every walk of life. Judith was co-ordinating that work from her desk in the press office. It helped that I had quietly seen to it that she had been promoted a couple of times and was now wielding quite a significant degree of influence in her own right.

Mere months after she came on board we had members in every department. Several in Roads and Transportation – I was very pleased with them when they started mooting the idea of a second Forth Road Bridge. That would cause real havoc. And there were not a few in Education. We were beginning, in a small way, to reach out. Implementing some reforms here, a restructuring there. People find it very unsettling, you know, having their whole lives upturned on the whim of some bureaucrat. It's amazing how much psychological damage you can do just by messing about with what goes on in a school classroom, and psychological damage is what you need when you're softening the populace up, readying them for their acceptance of you as their Dark Controller.

The way the network of evildoers was shaping up was a source of great satisfaction to me. Through myself, through Judith, and the various underlings we had recruited at the Scottish Office, we were beginning to exert a real influence in administration – which was soon to increase exponentially as more and more of the real business of government gravitated towards Edinburgh. Through Meek's evil offices, we were beginning to control people in other significant areas of life in the nation's capital. The justiciary, medicine, broadcasting for instance. We recruited from any profession where there is a high proportion of people who come into contact with mental health-care professionals acting in their professional capacity. We recruited any suitable candidates who came into contact with the machinery of governance, and anybody whom we knew socially (and Judith and I were both very well connected, remember, and Meek was very appealing).

Another thing occurred to me as I was dictating that bit about despair to the Grocer of Doom (referring to his own minutes of a meeting which took place a few months before) and thinking of Judith's work in the Press Office.

'Despair is my friend' – it's a ready-made American-style marketing slogan. A book and video with this title would be an enormous asset to us in trying to get our message across in the USA and the south-east of England (there is increasingly little difference). I see guest appearances on television chat shows with those awful Oprah and Donaghue and Vanessa people. They won't know they're helping the Forces of Darkness, of course. Or will they? Perhaps they will. It doesn't matter. The important thing is that getting on these TV programmes seems to be as easy as evacuating your lower intestine when your belly is full of sennapods. The people who watch them are *ipso facto* extremely gullible. Therefore, we gain access to a mass audience of willing converts. It's brilliant.

I feel quite pleased with myself.

Wait, though. There's more.

Self-help classes. I see my people running self-help classes. Show the plebs how to learn to accept despair. Befriend it. Reach out and embrace it and say hey despair, I love you, you're my friend. Sow an Evil seed in their hearts.

God. Listen to him. He's chuckling now. Like an idiot. And such a gloomy bastard the rest of the time.

It had long been my intention, once a sufficiently large number of apostles had been recruited, to set up working parties – two of them – to prepare the ground for the Implementation of Evil. Both groups would have a membership of six officers, plus myself in the chair. The Grocer would take notes for future reference.

One of the groups would be responsible for devising policy (working to a set of broad objectives defined and set out by myself in consultation with my Father) and the remit of the other would be strategy and procedure for implementation.

However, since the number of executive officers was smaller than had initially been anticipated due to a slight shortfall in recruitment, it was decided by myself in consultation with my Father, to combine the two functions and set up the joint working party on Procedures for Implementation, Strategy and Policy (PISP).

Membership of the PISP group was as follows: Myself (chair); Gillian Meek (Policy Officer); J X Heriot (officer responsible for Strategy and Implementation). The Grocer of Doom would take notes for future reference.

The first thing the PISP group did was, at my instigation, to draft a mission statement and strategy. This is it:

Our Goal is to bring about the Reign of Terror upon the Earth, that the Antichrist might have True Dominion over all the creatures that dwell thereupon.

Our Strategy is to create social instability, undermine society

*and the institutions which underpin it. We will do this by
spreading Evil like an epidemic through the land, creating
fear and injustice wherever possible.*

*Our immediate goal is to foster the necessary conditions for
our takeover in Scotland. It is from there that we shall spread
out and conquer.*

From the very start, the working party was very successful
as a forum for the generation of ideas. Both executive
officers exhibited a very healthy attitude and a great deal
of enthusiasm and, after only seven months (meeting on
the first and third Friday of every month), we had drawn
up a draft version of the first section of the Guidelines for
the Implementation of Evil. This draft was then circulated
more widely, amongst members of our growing network
of evil-doers and other relevant persons, for discussion. In
the meantime, the PISP group went on to start drawing
up the next section of the Guidelines.

I insisted that, for these meetings, the executive officers
wear short skirts. I arranged matters so that there was no
table in the meeting room, save the desk behind which I
sat, so they had to sit facing me in the open. This enabled me
to look at their legs. I noticed that Meek had a preference
for black hosiery, whilst Judith preferred sheer tan. I came
to the conclusion that, whilst there was much to be said in
favour of each, I, on the whole, preferred the latter. From
an aesthetic point of view.

I also liked watching them sitting next to each other.
They competed for my favours. There was a healthy rivalry
between them.

SIX-POINT RECRUITMENT PLAN

It seemed vital that, if Meek and Judith were to bring me basket cases and evil doers so that we could establish a network, we should have a recruitment policy. We had one at the Scottish Office, and the personnel department swore by it. I assumed the mantle of personnel officer myself, since it requires no special skills or training, and does not involve doing any work, and drew one up. It consists of six points which officers should look for in potential recruits and bear in mind.

1. All persons shall be considered eligible for membership of the network of evil-doers, regardless of age, race, religion or sexual orientation.

2. The most important quality we are looking for is a predisposition to evil. However, since this exists in almost all human beings, we need to define our objectives further.

3. We positively welcome applications from those with anti-social characteristics. The ability and desire to flout moral norms and conventions is an asset. Persons with this characteristic should be encouraged to point it out to the officers of the PISP group upon making their application.

4. We also positively welcome applications from hypocrites and exponents of moral cant. Previous experience in the church or any of the political parties is advantageous.

5. Frustrated egoists are more likely to be suitable for employment in the network than those with no ego at all. Constant thwartment of a powerful ego leads to many sorts of dangerous propensities which will be useful to us.

6. The presence of conventional-normatively unacceptable drives and impulses will also be a great asset to an applicant. Sociopaths, psychopaths, perverts and paederasts, provided they can be proved trustworthy, will all make excellent members of the network of evil-doers.

SO HOW EXACTLY DO YOU RECRUIT A MEMBER OF THE NETWORK?

It's really quite easy. You have to know what to look for in a person. It's often self-interest, but it could also be the glamour of evil, mistaken good intentions (you know what they say about the road to hell), boredom, lust, envy or any of a thousand other things which can snare you a new member.

I'll cheerfully admit that it's not everyone who can be recruited. Some people are sure of themselves, have a firm sense of right and wrong and are altruistic and incorruptible. There aren't very many of them though. I would put them at about 0.2% of the population. In Edinburgh, anyway. Amongst the right sort. The figure may be higher elsewhere. Or in other social classes.

Meek's very good at spotting potential recruits. She says it's something in the eyes. Sometimes, she says, it's a vacant expression. Sometimes it's sheer malice. Sometimes it's bewilderment, but all three betoken someone who's suitable for membership of the network. It was she who recruited the senior producer at the BBC, the two poets, the industrial architect and the director of social work. And all within a fortnight.

I don't know what use the poets will be.

ON YOUR KNEES, HUMAN SCUM

I have an ordinary speaking voice. In fact, some people used to tell me that it was quite drab, being monotone and uninflected even in moments of great excitement.

After my Revelation, however, I discovered that I have another voice. I wouldn't say that this other voice was my real voice, it is simply another. It sounds a bit like a dog barking, though it articulates human words (usually, obviously, in English but there is the occasional Latin tag). It is a very useful voice because it is great for giving orders, bending others to My Will.

The effect of the dog-voice is increased by the light which shines in my eyes when I use it. It glows red, like light shining through a bottle of blood, and gets redder the angrier I am. If I use the dog-voice to say 'On your knees and worship me before you die, human scum', the effect is one of enormous power. I have practised this in front of the bathroom mirror. The bathroom is internal and has no windows. Sometimes I switch the light off – there is only the one light, over the mirror, with a pull-cord – and watch my eyes shining in the blackness.

MIRROR, MIRROR, IN THE BATHROOM

Which reminds me of something which happened just after my first Revelation. I was getting ready for work the morning after this party, having a shave in front of the bathroom mirror. I looked down to wash some of the accreted whiskers from the blade of my safety razor, and when I looked back at my reflection through the steam rising from the washbasin, I saw Myself as I really was. I beheld Myself.

I had horns. My eyes were glowing red. There was a black star on my brow and I was surrounded by a host of dark angels who were praising me. 'Behold, Behold,' they were singing, 'the Lord of Darkness is awakened. His Day is nigh.'

In a moment the vision was gone, and I reappeared in the mirror in mortal guise. However, I now knew what I looked like on the inside.

This is a picture of what I looked like. I drew it earlier and made the Grocer stick it in with Pritt. It had better stay there or he's dead veg. I haven't drawn the ears on, because I can't draw ears. They were huge and pointy, and had great tufts of hair growing out of them.

The only things that remained once the vision had faded were an immense feeling of power, a few wisps of smoke and a slight goaty aroma.

DISCUSSION AND DISCONCERTMENT

After the first draft of the first section of the guidelines had been produced, the PISP group decided that it was time to begin the process of Implementation. The PISP group therefore discussed a number of issues to lay down the groundwork, and decided that it was now agreed that our first strategic goal should be the fostering of high levels of public discontentment, disconcertment and consternation tending to produce a general lack of confidence or spirit of anomie or alienation in accordance with Post-chaotic Procedures V of the guidelines: the encouragement of negative public emotional modality. In short, a general feeling that things were going to get worse.

The best way to set about achieving this, it was decided, would be to initiate some action or series of actions that was so gruesome and/or unsettling that the public would be outraged, and to maintain this pressure over a considerable period of time. Achieving the necessary impact would, of course, depend on our being able to generate the right kind of publicity. It was therefore decided that PISP would appoint a press and publicity officer.

There was then some discussion as to whether it would be better to recruit a press and publicity officer, or to make an internal appointment. It was eventually decided that the time-delay to the implementation process which the induction and training of a new officer would involve would constitute a considerable delay to the programme, and that it was therefore advisable, in the view of the group, to make an internal appointment.

There was then further discussion as to who should be appointed, but it was eventually decided that Judith should be given the post, as she had gathered the skills and experience necessary in the course of her work as Senior Press and PR Officer at the Scottish Office. She would take on this new role in addition to her own present duties, but would, of course, be able to offload some of the more routine aspects of these onto Meek or Myself should she find herself over-burdened.

The appointment was formally made and acknowledged, and Judith was congratulated by all present, though I noticed Meek frowning. The PISP group then decided to move on to discussion of the next stage of Implementation – identifying and developing a strategy which would enable us to achieve our initial objective: the enfosterment of high levels of public discontentment, disconcertment and consternation.

A range of options were discussed. One of these was the humiliation of significant representatives of church and/or state. In this category, PISP decided that one good way of furthering this aim, and a potentially rewarding one, would be to circulate stories about the Queen to the effect that she was sexually deviant in some way, possibly involving animals. A trained goat was mentioned in this connection. A more subtle approach outlined at this juncture was that we could spread the story that she smelt faintly of excrement, as you would notice if you met her at garden parties or similar functions.

These stories would gain much currency and credence as they would be circulated by those influential and/or prominent members of the Edinburgh establishment who were under our power, and by members of the network of evil-doers.

PISP was unable to identify any course of action which would have an unsettling effect on the church, as the members were unable to identify any sufficiently prominent churchmen, or anything interesting to say about them. This is one of the few negative aspects of living in a country with no established church.

At this point in the discussion it was decided that, though the spreading of damaging stories about prominent and semi-sacred public figures would be a good way of unsettling the public at large, some more substantive course of action would, nevertheless, have to be identified.

It was resolved that this would be the main business of the next meeting of PISP. We then proceeded to discuss the other main business on the agenda for the meeting, which was the implementation of an outreach initiative. Judith X Heriot, who had placed the item on the agenda, took the floor.

OUTREACH AND OUTRAGE

The basic idea behind the outreach initiative was that we should run a series of classes, tutorials and workshops to appeal to the public, to explain ourselves and, as she rather crudely put it, to mess with people's heads. All the fundamentalist churches do it, Judith said. As she explained it, the initiative was very attractive both as a means of recruiting more members of the network of evildoers and as a means of spreading Evil itself throughout the land.

There was, initially, some discussion of whether it would be best to advertise the outreach initiative explicitly as dealing with evil, or to adopt a more subtle approach. It was decided that this should be best left to the responsible officer, to be decided according to the circumstances operating at the time, but that, since circumstances in which either approach could be adopted could be envisaged, it would be as well to outline strategies for both.

In the event of the initiative being advertised openly as Evil, some very useful slogans emerged from the first few minutes of brain-storming. Amongst these were 'Learning to Love Evil', 'Loving Hate', 'Evil can be Good for you' and 'Help yourself by doing Evil'.

It began to emerge as the overwhelming feeling of the group, however, that it would, in the vast majority of cases, be safer to adopt a subtler approach. This would also make booking into local authority premises to run classes much easier. Judith agreed, and outlined a series of strategies she had already identified. Looking back on this, I remember being most impressed by her instinctive grasp of how to appeal to the public, and of the basic principles of marketing. She is, by far, the most skilled of all my many lieutenants and apostles in manipulation and deviousness.

She outlined a four-point plan, which would appeal to different segments of the public in various ways. Her first point was that, if we were being subtle, we should not actually use the term 'evil' but should make up some term which we knew was the equivalent, but which was, in the public perception, innocuous. She suggested 'Heptonism', as a tribute to me. I was quite touched.

She then went on to outline her four broad strategies, which were as follows:

1. Advertise classes in Heptonism (without ever mentioning the 'E' word, Evil) as a New Age Philosophy, along much the same lines as aromatherapy or transcendental meditation. This would appeal to weirdos and to the more adventurous (if not always the most well-educated) kind of housewife.

2. Stress the self-help angle – the Hepton way to self-reliance. These could, in fact, easily be the same classes as the New Age philosophy ones, only tailored to an even sadder, more angst-ridden audience.

3. Set up and advertise Heptonic bible readings and prayer groups. It would, Judith said, be simplicity itself to construct a message with which we agreed from biblical passages, and the emotive and psychological power of prayer (despite its lack of any other sort of power) was a very useful tool. Much of the ground, she said, had already been covered – it was only a simple step from right-wing Christian fundamentalism to outright belief in Evil, so we could appeal to the same people.

4. Set up counselling sessions in grief therapy, dealing with despair, coping with loss and loneliness etc, and introduce an element of evil into them.

Just as she'd finished outlining her plan, and I thought this was most impressive, she said that she'd just thought of something else and if we could bear with her a few moments she'd try to formulate it. Yes, here it was. Politics, she said. We were messing about with religion – politics is the other great Scottish bugbear. Making it up on the spot, she suggested that we could stage a few series of political meetings on topics like Why Scotland Must Be Ready to Stand Alone; Scotland in Europe – the Face of the Future?; Proud Heritage, What Future?. Stuff like that, anyway. It would be easy, she said. We'd advertise the meetings in the usual ways – fly posters, adverts in magazines, letting newspapers and listings magazines know. There were hundreds of nutters who would crawl out of the woodwork for stuff like that. All I'd have to do would be to turn on the charisma and speak persuasively and I've have them hooked. I shouldn't find it too hard, she said. I was always speaking like one of those nationalist loonies anyway.

I had to agree. It would work like a charm.

The beauty of the outreach initiative is that it's a way of reaching out into the mass of the populace. Most of our other strategies and almost all of our recruitment, thus far, had concentrated on the elite which runs the town (for good reasons – it runs the town, and he who controls Edinburgh controls the world) but I was conscious of a need to be moving forward, and for moving forward you need footsoldiers.

We agreed to implement these strategies immediately. Judith was given full responsibility. It would keep her busy, but we had every confidence in her abilities. She would report back to us on her progress, and could, at any time, call on us for assistance if the workload became too great, as we expected it might, as the network of evil doers grew and the number of outreach initiatives expanded accordingly.

I must say I was very impressed with this idea, and told Judith as much at the end of the meeting. I invited her out for dinner. 'Let's go to Martin's', I said, and I told Meek and the Grocer to clear away the chairs.

MALEFACTION AND MELON

In the time-lag between PISP meetings I was writing more of this book, and decided to experiment with some forms of Evil in action. I ran over a few possibilities in my mind. Something sexual, perhaps?

One could, I thought, cut or (preferably) rip the head off a tramp or, to be more politically correct, homeless person, and copulate with the severed neck. One could disembowel a dog and fellate its severed penis. But doing this sort of thing poses a number of problems. You might, for instance, enjoy it, which would make it merely Selfish. And then again, why bother? Doing it in public, of course, would create a disturbance and have some of the unsettling effect we were going for, but still . . .

It was worth a try. 'Hey, you. Grocer,' I said, 'off you go'.

It was, in fact, reasonably successful, especially given that it was the Grocer who did it. I was quite pleased with him for once.

He couldn't find a tramp. He obviously wasn't looking very hard because I always find hundreds of them whenever I walk down the street. This is partly due to the work of the

Scottish Office (unaided by myself, in this instance) and the city council, which have a policy of forcing poor people to live on the streets, getting in your way and bothering you for money when you're trying to go about your business or to the shops. But there's never one around when you want one. He found a dog, but then he realised that he couldn't hold it still enough to disembowel it and anyway he only had the paring knife which he uses for top-and-tailing root vegetables with him.

So he shagged a melon. This was, obviously, not as potent as killing something – sex and death is a potent combination – but sex and food is not bad.

He shagged it in Princes Street Gardens in front of a party of old dears and a primary school class who were on a nature ramble looking at squirrels. After he'd shagged it he ate it. All before the police arrived.

A formal complaint was made to them, and it made the papers. This is what one of them said: 'An unknown man is being sought by the police today after an incident involving a sexual act with a piece of fruit in Princes Street Gardens. Horrified onlookers stood transfixed as they saw the man produce a melon, cut a hole in it with what appeared to be a sharp fruit knife, and engage in the sexual act. Police were summoned but the man had absconded before they arrived. He was described by eye-witnesses as 'wizened'.'

'Well done,' I said to him when I read this. 'I am pleased with you today. But tomorrow it's back to misery again.' It was a small beginning, but we were just feeling our way. Mighty oaks from little acorns. Mighty melon trees from little melon seed.

How mighty is a melon tree?

I think I remember reading somewhere that melon plants

spread out horizontally and cover the earth, in much the same manner as strawberries.

How appropriate. A good vegetable metaphor.

Guidelines on the implementation of Evil

The Importance of Impersonality

1. Practitioner personality is not a prime principle.

2. Evil is, contrary to the popular conception, essentially an anonymous process.

3. Please bear in mind the distinction between wickedness, sociopathy and psychopathy on the one hand, and Evil on the other.

4. Wickedness, sociopathy and psychopathy are about personality. Think of Dahmer, Nielsen, Sutcliffe, Manson, West. Insignificant. Killed people, caused suffering to others, but achieved nothing.

5. Evil is about process, system, organisation. Think of Hitler, Stalin, Pol Pot. The important thing is not the personality of the practitioner, it is the systems for the implementation of Evil implemented by the practitioner.

The next meeting of the PISP group was devoted solely to identifying a course of action which would meet the specifications laid down at the previous session for a course of action which would have an unsettling effect on the public at large thereby generating disconcertment, discontentment and consternation. A number of possibilities were discussed.

It was suggested, for instance, that LSD be put into tins of dog food, causing dogs to behave strangely, giving rise to a rash of unexplained maulings, whimperings, involuntary excretions and sudden deaths. This would, it was argued, upset a nation of dog-lovers radically. This suggestion was rejected, however, on the grounds that it had not been established that LSD would work on dogs, and that we had, as yet, no access to a supply of the drug, or, indeed, to the dog food.

Similarly, the suggestion that we annoy the gardeners by irradiating all packets of seeds before they reach the garden centre was discounted as too elaborate given the minimal return of three million slightly miffed old dears and codgers.

Eventually a course of action was identified.

It was decided that a receptacle (as yet unidentified) containing an assortment of human body parts should be left in a prominent public place, along with a suitably worded note claiming responsibility for the action in My Name and that of My Father. This, PISP decided, would have an unsettling effect on the public. A letter would be written to a selection of newspapers explaining our actions, stating that this was the first stage in my taking over the world, and saying that people should expect much more of this kind of thing later on.

PISP discussed a range of options as to the appendages themselves: should the appendages be removed from living persons or dead, and if the latter, should those persons be already dead or killed expressly for the purposes of appendage-removal. There was also the question of the identification of the specific appendages to be included in the receptacle – legs, arms, or other body parts?

In the end, it was decided that these specific questions could be settled at the discretion of the executive officer in charge of the operation. It was also decided, at the suggestion of the chair, that the executive officer should be Gillian Meek. Part of my reason for suggesting her for the job was that she'd been looking a bit down in the dumps since Judith's success with the outreach idea. I got the distinct impression that she was just a tiny bit jealous, and I wanted to give her a bit of a boost.

HAVE A STIFF ONE ON ME

In any case, Meek was the obvious choice for the job. She had, after all, ready access to any number of dead bodies and discarded body parts. Even though the Royal Edinburgh Hospital is a psychiatric establishment, they still manage to lose their fair share of patients. People who are psychologically disadvantaged often have medical problems too. The corpses were, she had told us many times, left lying around in the hospital, often for weeks on end, and would sometimes turn up in the oddest of places. It would be a simple matter for her to collect the requisite number of appendages and smuggle them out of the hospital for the next stage of the operation.

Besides, Meek has a great feel for death. She likes dead people. She has a key to the mortuary, and often hangs around with them. Corpses are great fun, she says. Some of her best friends are dead. Admittedly, some of her worst enemies are also dead, as well as a lot of people who were just unfortunate in encountering her, but most of her mortuary friends were dead before she ever met them.

There are one or two things, she told me once, that most people don't know about corpses but which make them especially attractive to certain sorts of people.

Especially male corpses.

And especially to nurses.

If you were any less animated, you Turnip, you would look even more like a corpse. Might do you some good with a nurse.

This is what she told me. I have my doubts. It may have been another one of her nurse jokes, but she kept a straight face. The thing is, she said, there is one reason why all corpses are called stiffs, but there are two reasons why nurses call male corpses stiffs. It has to do with the gases which bloat up inside the reproductive organs. They get very swollen. Erect. If you think about it it's quite logical really. Instead of getting engorged with blood, they get engorged with gas. The effect is pretty much the same.

Anyway, there are, it seems, a number of nurses who look forward to the death of a male patient quite eagerly. They arrange to meet them in the mortuary a day or so after expiry. Sometimes it involves hanging around for a bit until the conditions within the genito-urinary tract of the deceased are just right, but it is, apparently, well worth the wait, especially for a really hunky one. Once he's up, he won't let you down. He can keep going for hours, and you don't get pregnant. They call it late-dating, or an after-the-sell-by beefcake.

Most female nurses, Meek says, have been out with at least one dead guy even if, like Meek, they work in areas where it is uncommon to come in contact with corpses, and most who try it really like it. Most of them keep a key to the mortuary secreted somewhere about their person. Competition for the best bits of after-the-sell-by beefcake is quite rigorous.

Anyway, that's the reason she was the man for the appendages job.

MEEK G, A CHARACTER PROFILE

Since we're talking about Meek I thought it might be useful to tell you a little bit more about her, since she is a trusted lieutenant.

The basic trouble with her, the reason she was so unhappy when I found her, was that she had no self-confidence. I'm no great expert on human psychology, but it seems to me to be obvious that someone who believed in herself would not have let herself be treated in that manner by all those sundry men in the medical-psychological profession. Especially given that she had something they wanted (even if some of them didn't want it all that much – she did have reputation as an easy lay).

This is something which, as a detached, non-regular-human being type observer, I've often noticed about girlies. Sorry, young women. They can be charming, witty, intelligent, attractive, but have the self-assurance of a teenager with a stammer, spots, and jam-jar spectacles. This, it often happens, is particularly true of those girlies who don't have regular or permanent men in their lives. I wonder why?

Mind you, to digress for a moment, there are some women who are charming, witty, intelligent, attractive and full of beans, brimming with confidence. Judith, for instance. Well, charming is not quite the right word. Not even close, in fact, but she is all of the other three, and has a definite way with her.

Most people, in their heart of hearts, think that women like Judith are absolute bitches.

I suppose this counts of proof, if any were needed, that women get a rough deal in life.

So do men though. I don't want to be sexist.

MEEK G, A CHARACTER PROFILE II

Sorry, I wandered off the point a little. I was about to tell you a bit about Meek to give you another insight into the nature of evil. A different perspective. A look at one of its most capable servants.

That first day I met Meek I went back to her flat. She had a one-room top-floor flat off Easter Road. The stair up to it was filthy. There were chip papers, lager tins, cigarette packets and old newspapers lying around, and it smelt of urine.

I saw Meek freeze when we got to the last flight of steps. I knew instantly what was wrong. She hadn't been expecting a visitor, and her flat was a complete tip. I said to her, 'Don't worry if the house is a little untidy, I won't mind.' She breathed a sigh of relief, and we continued up.

Once she'd opened the door and was halfway through, she turned to me and said, 'It really is a complete mess. Sorry.' She smiled. I reassured her: 'Never mind,' I said, 'you should see my place.'

'Yes,' she said, 'I'd like to.'

Even so, I wasn't quite prepared for the devastation which met my eyes on entering the flat. There was scarcely an inch of floor space visible. There was soiled underwear lying around, mixed up, as far as I could tell, with clean. There were dirty dishes on the table and on the floor, and used coffee cups on every available surface. The bed was unmade and the sheets stained.

As you looked more closely, you could begin to discern features of decoration amidst all the mess. There was, for instance, a poster on the wall advertising a film called Dick, which seemed to be about penises, and on the mantel shelf there was a small green bronze of a satyr with an engorged member. The word 'Crete' was written on the side of the plinth in quasi-Greek lettering.

It took a few minutes for her to rush around the flat, frantically clearing things away. It didn't make much difference, but at least there was now somewhere to sit down. We sat, with mugs of coffee, and we talked. It was then that I gave her the gift of self-confidence. It was a question of making her place some trust in me – it helps that I am obviously rich and am sexually attractive – and then telling her that I thought she was the most gorgeous creature I had ever seen. Something of the sort, anyway.

It took a while, obviously. You can't achieve a transformation like that overnight. But it was remarkable to witness the change in her. Physically she looked better, but that was nothing. She got her hair cut in what I believe is called a bob. You often find that girlies with their hair cut in bobs are bubbly, and you might well say the same of Meek. Before I increased her confidence by telling her one or two simple things, you would have described her as nice but mixed up, shy. But then, that was before she got her hair cut. She wore it long and straight, with streaks in it. The roots were darker than the rest.

Here's a mark of how bubbly she is now. About three weeks after we met, we were sitting in her flat, now spruced up and tidy, I asked her to dance the dance of the seven veils. She didn't have seven veils, so she made do with three silk scarves, a tea towel, a net curtain and a lace table cloth. She danced behind the bead curtain which separates the kitchenette from the rest of the flat, and that counted as the seventh veil.

She pulled it off most adequately. Very erotic. Even though the tea towel said *A Present from Troon* on it.

GUFFAW

Guffaw is perhaps overstating the case, but I like the fact that evil can hide in the mundane. In the humdrum. No-one would have guessed as I rode the 7, 11 or 37 down Leith Walk to the Scottish Office that I was the Antichrist. It

84

made me laugh, the fact that there I was, taking the bus to work, beavering away at the Scottish Office, nipping down to Meek's flat, all within a few square miles, a few square miles of the most unremarkable northern bits of the city. Leith, Easter Road, Regent Terrace. Dreich, Festering Slow, Full of Menace.

No-one would have guessed, had they been permitted access to my luxurious top-floor office in our swanky Victoria Quay headquarters, that I was the Embodiment of Evil. No-one would have guessed, had they seen me walking the four and a half minutes it took to get from my house down to the bottom of Calton Hill and along Easter Road to Meek's, that I was going to see my lieutenant and that together we were plotting the overthrow of the entire way of life we saw all around us.

It was a pity that Judith lived so far away in Morningside. Still, she was young and reasonably trendy, and she had money so that's where she lived. I imagine that she got a bit of a frisson contemplating the little people around her when she was doing her shopping in Safeway's.

I don't know, though. We didn't talk about it.

MEEK G, CHARACTER PROFILE III

Something I forgot to explain. Stupid really, because in context it's the most important thing. The thing about Meek which I suppose an outsider would find most remarkable is the fact that she is not, in herself, predisposed to evil. Unlike Judith. I genuinely believe that what she does she does out of devotion to me.

I'm not sure whether this is a good thing or not, but I have to admit to a bit of a glow.

Guidelines on the Implementation of Evil

The importance of planning

1. Evil is not something which can happen spontaneously.

2. Because it is a matter of system, process and organisation, it needs organisation itself.

3. It follows, therefore, that Evil must be planned in advance in order to be successfully implemented.

HECTOR'S HOUSE PARTIES

After some 13 months of more or less constant PISP activity, the network of evil doers had a full time membership of over 100, with many more part-time members and consultant evil-doers, many of them from the Scottish National Party and various fringe nationalist groups, thanks to a few meetings staged here and there in back rooms of pubs and the odd church hall. These ranged from housewives to lawyers to media personalities to junkies to policemen. Various recruitment strategies were tried, but, after a year, we were finding that the evil doers were coming to us. People talk, I suppose, and we were developing a reputation by word of mouth.

Our meetings were almost social gatherings. They were known as Hector's House Parties. Oh, we got down to business alright. We discussed strategies and I addressed them on the nature and theory of evil, but they could have been coffee mornings run by some titled lady (the one who lived next door, for instance) or charity events put on by one of Edinburgh's swankier churches (the one on Calton hill, for instance). Definitely no oiks. I had to send the Grocer out.

I had nothing but contempt for them, you know. They were the products of the best education money could buy – Loretto's, the Academy, Watson's, St George's, Mary Erskine – they were useful to me, and they were my kind socially, but they were so very small-minded. No vision.

Anyway, they started talking, to their intimates, and gradually word of the network spread and people started asking to join. As an example of the kind of thing that started to happen, let me tell you about a man who walked into my office one day. His name was Peter Pickford. I could tell what he wanted simply by looking at him. He was in his fifties, had grey hair and no neck.

He was not executive material, largely due to a lack of breeding and intelligence, but he was very gifted. He began to tell me about the mini Reign of Terror which he had established in his village: Balerno. He called it a village. I call it a suburb. But that's by-the-by. He was extremely litigious. He had sued almost all the adults living in the 'village', for such things as having building work done which did not quite match the details on the planning applications, or for keeping animals in contravention of some by-law or ancient statute.

But he also had far more creative ideas than that. He had a

gift for creating unnecessary and very intrusive noise, often with power tools.

He was a reasonably wealthy man, having made his money in scrap dealing. One of the things he used to do was buy up old buses and vans, several of them at a time, and leave them in the street, outside people's doors and windows, blocking the light and the view to the outside world. There was nothing illegal about this, even when he had more than thirty vans in the street at any one time. It drove the villagers to distraction.

I was very impressed. I offered him a position then and there, and he went on to do some very valuable work for the network.

He's dead now, more's the pity. The evil can turn in on you if you do not control it properly.

THE APPENDAGES

There were seven of them. Six arms and a leg. All left.

Meek brought them to me one Thursday evening in October at about six-thirty, when she'd just knocked off her afternoon shift. They were in various states of decay, but that was perfectly alright for our purposes as we were going for all-out horror and shock value rather than the uniformity of appearance that, for instance, a young visual artist at one of the London galleries might have been looking for.

The limbs were stuffed into a black plastic bag with 'City of Edinburgh Council Refuse Disposal' written on it. This again was fine. The nature of the receptacle containing the appendages was mere incidental detail, though I suppose that we could have done without the 'Improving Services, Creating Jobs' logo and the prohibition on hot ashes and unwrapped broken glass. Nothing is ever perfect though, and I dare say that there were odd little annoying things which have grated on the nerves of the perpetrators of all the great acts of history – the shoddiness of Christ's sandals, Hitler's inability to get his moustache just so, etc.

There was an envelope in my pocket containing a note which read 'Tremble ye and behold for He is coming, and He is the Beast'. It was a trifle archaic in the way it expressed the imminence of my Reign of Terror, but there is a way of doing these things and you have to stick to it. Anyway, it said all that I wanted to say quite efficiently, with no ambiguity.

We'd had some debate about whether to put the note in the bag with the limbs or attach it somehow to the outside of the bag. There were arguments in favour of both options, but in the end we decided that the note might go unnoticed if we put it in the bag. This was the reason for the roll of sellotape which sat in my pocket beside the envelope.

We put the bag onto the back seat of my car, and drove around the city looking for a suitable place to deposit it. I told Meek that what we were looking for was a place like the bag itself – it looked 'armless but on closer examination wasn't. She laughed at my witticism, but without the enthusiasm I had expected.

We drove past the castle and St Giles. It wasn't the tourist season, so no-one would care about an off-putting discovery there. We briefly considered the City Chambers and then we drove on down the hill, past the new Parliament Building. But these were already places of iniquity, so the impact of the limbs would be lessened.

In the end we chose the entrance to a children's playground in Roseburn, reasoning that the discovery of the limbs would be much more likely to get the kind of reaction we were looking for if a child or, perhaps even better, a young mother pushing a pram, did the discovering. This was, we thought, a nice touch to round off an already brilliant scheme.

We parked by the side of the road. There was one hairy moment when a police car came past and slowed down – the involvement of the constabulary would have been an administrative headache so we took steps to avoid that contingency by pretending to be necking. Once the danger was past, I got out of the car and struggled with the bag (seven limbs, six arms and a leg, being quite heavy) until I had finally manoeuvred it onto the pavement outside the playground. I got back into the car and we drove off, smiling, pleased with a job well done, and doubly pleased at last to have made a real start on the task of bringing about my Reign of Terror. We chuckled at the thought of the publicity we would get in the papers and maybe even on TV the next day.

NO NEWS IS NOT ALWAYS GOOD NEWS

The papers the next day, however, made no mention of our Bag of Limbs. I was disappointed until I realised that the discovery had probably taken place too late to meet the news deadlines and, in any case, most newspapers are written well in advance of the news. I resolved to swallow my disappointment and wait until the next day, the Saturday, when there was bound to be a big fuss and front page headlines.

I took Judith out for lunch on the Friday, in her capacity as press and publicity officer, to ask her advice on whether we should be contacting the newspapers ourselves in order to let them know of what was happening. We went to the Caledonian Hotel. The office paid.

Judith's advice was that, in her opinion, there was little that could be done at this point, and that we had rather gotten ourselves into a situation where the success of our enterprise depended on the limbs being discovered, on the discoverer reporting the discovery to the police, and on the police letting the press know. She added that it would probably have been a good idea to consult her on our approach to the media before embarking on the exercise, rather than now, when it was too late.

On the whole, I thought, her tone was rather negative. She was distinctly frosty. I had to admit that she was right, though.

THE PAST REVISITED

My heart missed a beat on the Saturday when I saw the PM IN ARMS ROW headline on the front page of the Scotsman. However, the story made no mention of me, Edinburgh, or the Bag of Limbs — it was some tedious rubbish about the Middle East. There was no mention of us on Monday either, so I convened an extraordinary meeting of PISP for later that week.

In the meantime, I commanded Meek, when she got

off work at six-thirty that evening, to drive me back to the scene of our crime.

We arrived at the entrance to the playground. There was no sign of the bag. It must, then, have been discovered, so why no mention of it in the papers? Perhaps I had underestimated my enemies, and they were deliberately keeping it quiet in an attempt to thwart me. But their attempts would come to nothing. This was a minor setback.

A woman was passing. I engaged her in conversation.

'Excuse me,' I said. 'Do you come here often?'

She looked past me at something or somebody behind me and shouted, 'Jim! Jim! This weirdo's botherin' me.'

'No, no,' I reassured her. 'No, I wanted to know if you live around here.'

She started to shout again, but Meek got out of the car and said, 'It's OK', at which the woman's expression softened slightly. Meek is very good at putting people at their ease. You have to be in her profession.

'Oh,' the woman said. 'Aye, I stay just over the road there. That's ma man, standin by the door,' she added.

'The thing is,' I explained, 'we've lost something. We think we might have left it here last Thursday.'

'Oh?' she asked.

'Yes,' I said. 'Big thing, maybe left it sitting right there, where you're standing.'

'Oh,' she said. 'What d'it look like?'

'Black plastic bag,' I explained. 'Oddly shaped, large.'

'Thursday night, aye?'

'Yes,' I replied.

'Black plastic bag?' she asked.

'Yes, that's right,' I said.

'Bin bag?' she asked.

'Why, yes it was,' I said. 'Why?'

'Bin men come Friday mornings' she said. 'Mebbe you'd best speak tae the cooncil.'

APPRAISING APOSTLES BY THEIR APPEARANCES, AND OTHER QUALITIES

I've often paused to consider the basic differences of character between Meek and Judith. I spend a lot of time going over the two of them in my mind. They both have their qualities, and I can see the good points of both of them.

This is the strange thing. Although Judith is most like me, she isn't my favourite. This is actually quite confusing in some respects. I would have expected the reverse to be the case. You're supposed to be attracted to people who are like yourself, a psychologist once told me. It confuses me, I don't understand it, it worries me.

I'm also aware that there's a danger of my preferences interfering with the way I try to run the network, but I am most rigorous in my efforts not to let my favouritism show. Also, the mere fact that Meek is my favourite doesn't blind me to the fact that there are some jobs for which she is not the best person. I try to judge both of them on their merits.

Meek was, as I've tried to explain, once very mild mannered, very shy, very lacking in confidence. Now, though, she's bright and bubbly. She is very good with people (she once described herself as a 'people person'), though it is true that she is learning to take delight in causing people anguish. It seems to me that this might, perhaps, be because she spent so long caring for them in hospitals, holding their hands, making their beds, speaking to their relatives, cleaning up their shit, and it all got too much for her. A lifetime's frustration finding expression. She's full of fury. A seething, boiling mass of anger and resentment. That's what I mean when I say she's bubbly.

Judith, on the other hand, is more your classic ice-maiden. She never smiles or looks sad, never laughs, never cries. She is, though, what you might call 'glamorous', with her long blonde hair always tied back in a plait, and good looks. She exploits these qualities ruthlessly. People want her, and she knows it, and she found quite early on that her looks, combined with her undoubted subtlety and guile, could get more or less anything she wanted. People, men, are in awe of her because she's so attractive yet so forbidding.

Here's another curious thing: she's a bit like this with me too. Although we share much, although she is a trusted lieutenant, although I do not doubt her love of Evil, I do not feel that I know her very well. She is not a great one for the heart-to-heart talk. She has told me very little about herself. Nothing that she did not want me to know. The only thing she's ever volunteered to me is that she doesn't like talking about herself, and she doesn't like being talked about. Sometimes, when you look into her eyes, you can tell that there is no human warmth there. No fire. No personality, perhaps. No spark. Beneath her icy exterior there beats a heart that's twice as cold. This makes her an expert and dangerous practitioner of evil.

But Meek's a much better shag. I mentioned this to Judith, in a spirit of enquiry, just before I told her about the bag of limbs at that lunch at the Caledonian. She didn't take it at all well. I hadn't meant to offend her. I was simply wondering whether she could explain it to me.

It took me ages to mollify her. She was still being rather abrupt when we left. I got a taxi back to the office from the rank outside the hotel, and I held the door open for her but she said that she'd rather walk, thankyou very much. All the way down Princes Street and up Leith Walk. And it was raining.

LOST LIMBS

We sent the Grocer of Doom out to search the council refuse tip for the Bag of Limbs. He was gone for a very long time. I was beginning to hope that he would never return and, whilst this would mean that we had lost the limbs, we would never have to put up with him again and it would be a small price to pay.

He came back though.

Too right I came back pal. I was going to kill you. I was fucking seething. Millions of fucking bags I fucking searched through for you you bastard and not one word of thanks. You fucked up not me. Millions of the fucking things. Stupid fucking bag of limbs. Whole fucking thing was a stupid idea.

He came in filthy and stinking. He was covered in filth and ordure, not that it was easy to tell, eh Turnip? and there was more than a hint of rotting fish about him. Mingled, of course, with decay. He's never very attractive, but that night he surpassed himself. Odorous and odious. Malevolent and malodorous.

He said that he'd searched 5,200 bags and had seen no sign of any limbs. Now tell me, who's going to keep a count of 5,200 bags of refuse? A worthless lump of decaying vegetable matter, perhaps, but who in their right mind would do that? Personally, I don't think it's possible to search that many bags properly and efficiently. I know I would get very fed up and give up after 25.

THE GROCER: WHY?

I spend hours tormenting that turnip. I'm tormenting him now, making him write this down. It's even a kind of torment to talk to him about tormenting him. It's like when I was at school and I used to catch crane flies, except that I haven't pulled his legs off yet, and he has no wings. I play with him as a cat would with a captured shrew.

Sometimes I promise him things. I don't deliver.

Sometimes I belittle him in front of the others. I know he has the hots for Meek.

There, I've just done it again.

Sometimes I cause him physical pain. Sometimes I threaten to banish him from My Presence.

Why does he put up with this? He is a greedy creature, mean-spirited and desperate for the morsels I throw him. He is compelled by the magnetism of My Evil. He cannot escape, however hard he tries.

Besides, if he defied me (not that there is the remotest possibility of him finding the will to do that) he knows that I would destroy him.

If I could be bothered.

I had, as I say, hastily convened an extraordinary meeting of PISP that Friday. As it was, I had to go out in the morning to attend to some business at the office and I was late getting back, though I had left the Grocer with instructions to let the others in should this prove to be the case.

I was not at all prepared for the scene which met my eyes on my return. I was in a foul mood. I always was when I'd spent any time in the office. My mood was hardly helped by what confronted me when I returned. There was a definite air in the room. I asked the Grocer what was amiss, but he said nothing. Then I noticed that Judith was nursing her left eye and that a couple of her hairs were slightly out of place. Then I noticed that Meek also looked a bit dishevelled. Then I noticed that one of the pot plants had been knocked over and hastily put back in place. There was still earth on the floor.

'What's been going on?' I said. I was quite calm. I didn't use the Voice, even though I was tempted.

It took a while to extract an answer, but eventually Meek told me that Judith had attacked her with the umbrella plant. Judith said that was a lie and Meek said no it wasn't. Judith said 'you bitch' and went for Meek and I had to restrain her forcibly.

When I asked what it was all about they were strangely silent. I decided not to pursue the matter then and there as we had more important things to attend to, but I made it plain that I wanted no more of it, whatever it was.

We then moved on to the Bag of Limbs fiasco. I absolved all the officers involved of any responsibility for its relative failure. I say 'relative' because, as I said at the time, despite our failure to achieve our prime objectives of press coverage and public disconcertment, we did emerge from the affair somewhat the richer, not least in terms of wisdom and experience. 'Let's agree,' I told them, 'to say no more about this regrettable incident. We will re-implement the plan, starting again from scratch, taking into account all that we have learned over these past few days, and look upon these recent events as a dry run for our moment of glory.'

Deep down inside I was fuming, a boiling mass of rage, resentment and violence. It made a change from the normal misery, I suppose. I wanted to destroy them all, subject them to everlasting torment, but if there's one thing I have learned in all my years in the public sector, it is that the key to effective person-management lies in knowing when to make concessions. Besides, there was still an atmosphere about the room, and I thought it best to calm everybody down.

PRESS OFFICER MATERIAL

I know I've said that Judith has a cold heart and an icy exterior, but she does not always appear so. She is a woman of many guises. She can be very engaging when the occasion demands, or when it suits her, rather. She adopts roles depending on what will best serve her interests. She slips into them as other people slip into their clothes.

I can't help thinking that one of the reasons she is able to do this is that she has very little personality of her own. She has just two traits, as far as I've noticed: a huge, very sensitive ego which prickles somewhat if she thinks you're belittling her in some way, and a driving ambition. Apart from this, if she has got a personality, she keeps it well hidden. She has never shown it to me, in any case. This is what makes her so good at being a press officer.

As an instance of her gift for role-playing, let me tell you about her more than passable imitation of a caring, sympathetic person, the sort of person you'd want to tell all your troubles to. There was one occasion, she told me, where she played this role at a dinner party. The hostess (who was also called Judith) became distraught when the two of them were alone, and our Judith put on her caring persona and asked what was the matter. It all came out – the hostess was having an affair with her husband's best friend, and she didn't know what to do. She loved both of them and was terribly confused. Judith was very sympathetic until she was sure that she had heard all the details, including dates and times. Then she said 'you know, it could be much worse'. The hostess asked what she meant, and Judith said 'well, I could blackmail you. If you don't do certain favours for me, I'll tell your husband what you've been doing'. She has led me to believe that considerable material advantages accrued to her as a result of this conversation.

She's also a great one for exploiting her femaleness. She can claim, quite cynically, to be a victim of the machinations, conspiracies, repression, oppression, chauvinism, brutality, and emotional violence of certain men. It is not as if she is really a champion of women's rights, of course. I have seen her trample on people she has called 'sister' not a week before, if they get in her way, and never mind the undoubted fact that she is better at machinations, conspiracies, repression, oppression, etc than many of the people she accuses. It is just that she finds this sort of complaint a very effective means, in certain circumstances, of getting her own way. It was particularly effective, as it happens, in the public sector. Most public sector organisations are, quite rightly, very concerned about this sort of thing, but it leaves them wide open to abuse. Judith is just the sort of person to abuse them.

Other roles she can play with ease and apparent conviction include: suburban housewife (she's not married, but she can look like a harmless and boring stereotype when she wants to); little girl lost (a way of getting people to help her by appearing totally out of her depth before she stabs them in the eye); well-read brain-box (definitely appeals to a certain sort of man, whilst others, and some women, find it intimidating); socialite (she can mix it with the best of them, though she is incapable of taking any pleasure in this); woman of the people, quoting from The *Sun*, for the sake of cultivating common ground with, for instance, the people who come to her outreach sessions); woman of mystery (a charming, seductive and alluring presence).

Maybe it's not fair to complain about the lack of fire in her. I suppose that, if you can do all of these things, you don't really need a character of your own.

Besides, she has done us sterling service.

APPENDAGES: APPENDIX I

It took Meek three months to gather the wherewithal for another attempt to execute the appendages plan. I took it as a sign that things were going well that, again, when the limbs had been gathered there were once again seven of them, six arms and a leg, all of them left.

This time we took steps to ensure that the mistakes of the first attempt were not repeated. For a start, the limbs were placed in a box rather than a bin-bag, and all the writing on the box (it had contained a flat-packed kitchen unit from B&Q) was obliterated with a heavy felt-tip marker pen. Secondly, to be absolutely certain that the council's refuse collection operatives would not interfere with the plan, Meek telephoned the council in advance to ascertain precisely when the refuse collections were made from the site we had identified (the playground in Roseburn as before – we saw no reason to change it).

To ensure that the contents of the box were discovered, we arranged it so that there was a £20 note sticking out of the top as a lure. A lure.

Did you get it right that time, veghead?

And to ensure that the limbs were reported, Judith had done a brilliant job of telephoning three or four journalists repeatedly, not telling them who she was but merely saying 'isn't it about time you went out on a limb?' She felt that this would both excite their interest and ring a bell a few days later when our little treasure trove was discovered.

I was expecting another failure but, to my surprise, this time it went without a hitch.

The media response was, in fact, most gratifying. I felt quite cheerful for a few minutes. Well worth the wait, you might say, but nothing worthwhile is worth waiting for. There were front-page stories in all the Scottish newspapers, ranging from the bottom end of the market:

TINY TOT FINDS SHOCK IN BOX

to the top:

Body parts probe in Edinburgh.

We even got onto the television news, though the BBC took a rather sober line. The newsreader, introducing our item, said:

'Lothian and Borders Police are today trying to establish the origin of a box of limbs found at the entrance to a children's playground in Edinburgh early this morning.'

Since it is the television news which was the most influential, and which will almost always be most influential in any future incident of this nature, I shall quote the report in full. It went on thus: a reporter called James Matthews was standing outside the playground, speaking to camera:

The limbs, six arms and a leg, all of them left, were discovered in a cardboard box believed to have once

contained flat-packed kitchen units from a major DIY chain. They were found at 10.30 this morning by a three-year old toddler and his mother as they were entering this playground
[shot of children playing on swings and slide]
to meet other youngsters and young mothers. Neither the toddler nor his mother have been named by the police. A police spokesperson said that the limbs did not appear to have been reported as mislaid, but said that he found it difficult to envisage them having found their way to the playground entrance accidentally. It seemed, he said, much more likely that they had been placed there deliberately with the intention of having a child find them.
[cut to reporter speaking to camera]
The police spokesperson went on to describe the incident as
[looks down at notes]
'sickening'
[looks back at camera]
and said that the police would investigate the incident as a matter of the utmost priority. He said that they did have one or two leads to go on, including a note which had been found with the limbs, the text of which he read out to a news conference earlier this afternoon. The note said
[looks down at notes]
'Behold ye and tremble, for He is coming and He is the Beast. It'll get worse, you know'.
[looks back at camera]
The meaning of this message is, however, unclear. Anyone having any information about the incident is

asked to contact Inspector Gordon Allan of Lothian and Borders Police.

Guidelines for the Implementation of Evil

On the Earthly authorities

It is understandable that many newcomers to the enpractisement of Evil should find themselves concerned about possible future entanglements with the Earthly authorities during the course of their activities. However, the Earthly Authorities, in reality, present no great obstacle to even the most inexperienced practitioner of Evil. There are a number of reasons for this:

- I am all powerful, and shall watch over my followers
- ditto my Father, only more so
- the average representative of the Earthly Authorities is extremely narrow minded and cannot conceive of true evil, for all the sick and perverted things he sees in his work
- we, like the Lord, move in mysterious ways. This makes it hard for the authorities to keep tabs on us.

For these, and other, reasons, Practitioners must not be alarmed, disconcerted or in any other way unsettled by the activities of the Earthly authorities.

There are, of course, a number of practical measures which the Practitioner can undertake for him or her self. These include:

- not giving his or her name to the Earthly authorities
- ditto address
- staying well clear of the Earthly authorities wherever possible
- exercising circumspection and discretion in his or her dealings with non-practitioners and not telling them anything important

By these means, the Earthly authorities can be sidelined completely, allowing Evil to be practised with confidence and security.

PORK

It was at about this time, the time of our first major success, that the next of my apostles appeared to me, though I didn't recognise him as such at first. On The Night of the Bag of Limbs, having serviced Meek – yes Turnip, I serviced her, I did it to her until she was sore, then I did it to her some more. At her flat. She loves it. Then I went home and retired to bed. I was, to an extent, excited, so I slept fitfully, and I had a dream.

Ned Sherrin was in it. I don't know why it was Sherrin. I do not often dream of 1960s television and stage producers, but on this occasion I did. I believe the detail of the dream, the fact that it was Sherrin etc, to be irrelevant, but I report the facts as they occurred for the sake of accuracy.

He was dressed as Queen Victoria and professing a lack of amusement, as people who are dressed as Queen Victoria always do. This too, I believe, is irrelevant, though it struck a chord with me. What was important was that on his lap there was a huge ginger cat. I paid it no attention at first, but then I looked down and noticed it properly.

I saw that it was no ordinary cat. Instead of claws, for instance, it had human toes, and it was treading the soft folds of Sherrin's dress with these. There was also something human about its face, or at least about its lips and its large, slightly hooked nose. It had black hair growing in ringlets at the side of its head, which lent it an almost rabbinical air. It was smiling, but malevolently. Then it stuck out its tongue, which was green, and rolled back its eyes so that you could only see the whites. Its head went round the full 360 degrees.

I was so startled by this that I woke up. I was even more startled when I opened my eyes to see that same cat, sitting on my bedside table, glowing gingerly, still smiling. Then it spoke to me.

'Pork,' it said. Then it disappeared.

I had no idea what it meant.

SEX

It is something which crops up from time to time. Quite a lot actually. You might think that the Antichrist would have no need of sex, but I have urges. I have needs. There is an animal lust inside of me. It feeds on my gloom and grows stronger.

I am far more inventive in this field than humans, and I have far more power. It is one of the areas where my Immensity is most manifest.

It is always different for me, depending on which person I am venting my lusts on. I can make them melt away into nothing, or I can make them die when I take them. I can send them to Hell, or I can allow them to share, for a few brief seconds, in some of My Power.

With Meek, sex is a form of worship. She will do anything for me. Sometimes I like to get her to take my manhood in her mouth, working it up and down, and put the tip of it on the back of her tongue, on the place that makes you retch. She does it until she vomits. I like this because we both come in her mouth at the same time. Sometimes I get off again when she licks the vomit from my groin.

With Judith I've noticed a distinct cooling off since those early days in the toilets at work, which tends to suggest that she was never all that enthusiastic. Just playing a role, as usual. Maybe she no longer feels a need to impress me, having been promoted at work and having achieved influence in the network of evildoers. She tends nowadays just to lie back and think of – what? I wonder. I have no idea. Herself, probably.

TORQUIL

The next night I had the dream again. There were subtle differences – this time Sherrin was dressed as Boadicea and professing a hatred of Romans – but it was substantially the same dream. The cat was there again.

This time it spoke to me in the dream.

'Oy gevalt,' it said, shrugging and rolling its eyes heavenwards.

I looked at it. It was smiling horribly, though it kept its green tongue and the whites of its red eyes to itself.

'Oy oy oy' it said. 'You there, in the bed, wake up already.'

I did. The cat was, once again, sitting on my bedside table, glowing slightly.

'Hello,' I said.

'What joy, you're awake,' he replied – he had a masculine

voice, so I knew he was a he. The voice was a mixture of miaow and sarcasm.

He introduced himself. 'My name is Torquil,' he said. 'For my sins I've been sent here to help you.'

'Sent here?' I asked. 'By whom?'

'*Whom?*' the cat mocked, 'whom, is it? By your Father, that's who. I am His messenger, though I am also yours to command. To command already. Ha.'

'I see you do not care for the conventional niceties of social interaction, nor, indeed, for the employment of syntactical correctness,' I observed. 'But welcome anyway.'

'Thankyou so much,' he replied.

We sat and observed each other for many minutes, and I grew very curious about him. 'May I ask you a question?' I said.

'You just did,' he replied.

'No, I mean a personal question.'

'If you feel you must.'

'Torquil? I hope you'll forgive me for asking this, as I know that sometimes people can get offended by this sort of thing and indeed I've never felt really comfortable with it myself, but isn't Torquil a rather strange name for a being of so obviously, if you don't mind me saying so, Semitic an aspect?'

'Semitic schemitic,' he said. 'Who cares? What difference does it make? What's in a name? I am what I am, that's all.'

'I see,' I said though, in truth, I didn't. 'But you are, if you don't mind me asking, Jewish?'

'Mind? Why would I mind? What's to mind? You think I'm Jewish, OK I'm Jewish.'

'But I don't understand,' I said. 'I thought I was the

Antichrist. You know Anti Christ. I thought we were working within a distinctly Christian framework here'.

'Christian, Jewish, Buddhist, Muslim,' he said, 'what's the difference. Evil is evil. All the rest is so much bullshit.'

'I see,' I replied.

There was a long silence.

Then I said, 'Fancy a bowl of Kit-e-Kat?'

'Is it kosher?' he asked.

'What?'

'Just a joke,' he said. 'But thankyou, no. I have no need of mortal sustenance, though it was kind of you to ask.'

CONGRATULATIONS, AND CELEBRATIONS

The day after our big hit in the news – and they were still talking about us – I decided that I should reconvene PISP to give the team my personal congratulations, and to thank them for a job well done. I knew from my experience of work that this kind of thing can be very motivating for one's underlings. I had been on a management course once, and they told us this very thing.

I gathered them to me in a pub on the High Street. The World's End. The Grocer was not there. I saw no reason to lower the tone. I was planning to buy the girls some lunch, and I didn't want to put them off their food. The sight of him shovelling beans into his mouth with a spoon is not one of the most appealing.

It was an informal meeting: there was no agenda, no minutes, no formal structure. It was a Saturday, after all. All I wanted to do was pass on my congratulations, and thank Meek for assisting me with the operational aspects of the plan, and to thank Judith for ensuring that we got media coverage. She told me that all she had done was place telephone calls to a couple of reporters, but I said that this in itself was no mean feat. You had to know who to ring, what to say, and besides, even speaking to these people is a terrible ordeal. It was a very valuable contribution to our achievement.

My other reason for meeting them together like this was to find out how they would feel about a spot of three-in-a-bed sex.

SO HOW DID THEY FEEL ABOUT A SPOT OF THREE IN A BED SEX, THEN?

There was a hint of reluctance. Especially from Judith.

I don't know. Meek's more giving, as I've said before. More sexual. More sensual. More womanly. More open. Judith received the suggestion with a touch of contempt, but I persuaded her.

Part of the problem, I think, was her ambivalence towards Meek. She respects Meek as a fellow member of the network of evildoers, of course, but I can't help thinking that she sort of resents her as well. I think it's because of Meek's womanly qualities. Despite the fact that Judith is more powerful in evil, and is more conventionally good looking, she is jealous of Meek.

The sex itself was quite good from my point of view, though I had twice the usual post-coital melancholia.

It was a bit awkward at first. Everyone was a trifle

inhibited, but Meek took control and led us to the bed and undressed us all. She told me later that a threesome was something she'd always wanted to do. She really got off on it and quickly became the centre of the action. She lost herself completely, sitting on top of me, arching her back, as Judith and she stroked and kissed each other. Her cheeks were red and her lips more swollen than I'd ever seen them before, and she moaned like an animal. She shuddered and climaxed about seven times, and I think even Judith experienced a mild throbbing sensation. She let out a little squeak at one point, though she was strangely quiet and embarrassed afterwards.

Thinking of it as a sports fixture, I would have to say that Meek came first. I was a good second, and Judith showed some potential but was really playing out of her league. Like Raith Rovers.

A MESSAGE FROM ON HIGH

That night, Torquil appeared again, in the manner which I was coming to recognise as his usual mode of operating. He first appeared in my dream, this time arguing with the television and radio personality Robert Robinson over whether it was Plato or Democritus who represented the pinnacle of achievement in ancient Greek thought. I kept trying to interject that it was Aristotle, but they couldn't hear me or wouldn't listen, and I was growing increasingly desperate, but then Torquil turned and looked at me and said 'Butt out, Goy, this is not for you.'

This struck me as unfair both because I was fairly sure

that Robinson was himself a gentile, and because I knew I was right about Aristotle. However, Torquil appeared to be most insistent so, suppressing my resentment I bided my time until I began to drift out of the dream.

I awoke, and found him, as I had before, sitting on my bedside table, glowing. He was shaking his head and looking at me in what I interpreted as a downcast manner. He told me that he had brought me a message, as if he didn't have troubles enough already.

'From whom?' I asked.

'Whom? From your Father is whom, Mr Enunciation,' he replied.

'Look,' I said, 'let's not fight. Let's try and get along with one another. I shall,' I promised, 'when conversing with you, attempt to modulate my instinctive command and use of the correct grammatical construction of the language, in the hope of avoiding any unnecessary aggravation on your part.'

'Yes,' he said, 'you're right. Thank you. Me, I'll try in future not to be so tetchy at the way you speak. It won't be easy. You'd drive anyone crazy, but I'll try. I'm sorry, it's not your fault. I've had a bad day.'

There was a pause in which we regarded each other with something approaching warmth.

'You said you had a message,' I prompted him after a few minutes.

'Oh yes,' Torquil answered. 'That's right. Your Father is, you can imagine, a very busy man what with this and that, but he's very interested in what you're doing. 'Keep an eye on our boy for me', he tells me. 'I should keep an eye on him?' I said to him. 'Why should I keep an eye on him when he's more powerful than I am already? I've got so much to do here. He should be looking after me, maybe come down here and do some of my work.' 'Just do as I command,' he says. Shouts, more like. A blast from Hell. He's not to be argued with when he's in this mood, so here I am, keeping an eye on you. He told me to tell you he was very pleased, and to give you this message.'

There was a roll of thunder. Torquil cleared his throat, preparing to speak in a reverent, solemn tone, and as he did so the sky darkened, plunging my room into a gloom which was lightened only by the brief, harsh glare of lightning flashes. There was a deafening roar and a huge flash of light.

'The message is,' Torquil intoned, 'Keep up the good work.'

I let this sink in for a few minutes, and, when I had come to terms with the awesome magnitude of what had happened, I asked Torquil if he would be seeing my Father at any point in the near future. He said that it was entirely possible.

'In that case,' I said, 'I would be grateful if you would convey to Him my thanks for His support. I shall be passing it on to my staff and I am sure that it will prove an invaluable source of encouragement to them to know that their work is being appreciated at the very highest level.'

Later on something rather startling struck me. I remembered that, when I had been working there for around seven years, the Queen and Duke of Edinburgh had come to our office on a tour. The Duke had spoken to me. He shook my hand, limply, and said, 'Keep up the good work'.

I do not know what the significance of this is, but it's a strange coincidence.

I decided, for the present, to keep Torquil's existence a secret from the members of the network. It might, I thought, cause some resentment on their part if they knew that I thought his advice and support to be as valuable as theirs. Nevertheless, it seemed to me that it was important that they should know of my Father's approval of our activities, so I decided to convene an extraordinary meeting of the entire network, or at least of those who were free and could fit into the hall of my house.

'I have,' I told the assembled officers and members, 'received some very good news. My Father has communicated with me, and has told me that he is very pleased with those actions which we have carried out so far, and has urged us to keep up the good work. I regard this, I must say, as a very positive development indeed.' There was a round of applause. Several members nodded enthusiastically. One shouted 'Hurrah!'

I stared him down. 'The honourable gentleman forgets that he is not in the debating chamber now,' I said. He looked sheepish and cleared his throat.

One of the officers asked whether my Father had communicated with me personally, and I explained that, being the Fount and Origin of all Evil, just as I was its Earthly Embodiment, He was very busy – too busy to make personal appearances in all but the most exceptional of circumstances. He had though, I went on to say, sent me a personal message.

There was some danger, at this point, of Torquil's existence being exposed prematurely. Luckily, however, one of the officers asked a question about the precise relation, in terms of Evil, which existed between myself and my Father. I was able, with the aid of a flipchart and a marker pen, to explain it thus:

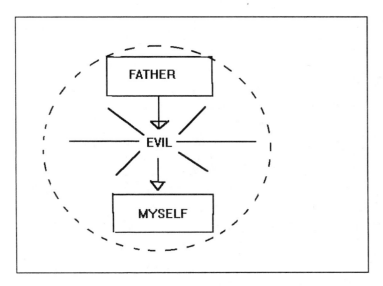

Obviously, I did the diagram on the spur of the moment, but it looked a lot more professional than this – even though I made the Grocer spend a good three hours drawing this out for you. The effect was pretty much the same. You get the idea.

This led, quite naturally, to a discussion of the nature of My Earthly Role. I was able to illustrate this using a diagram too. I had in my head a sort of military analogy. I said at the time that you might think of my Father as the sort of President of a country, and Myself as the supreme commander of its armed forces. If we were an army, I said, this is what we would look like:

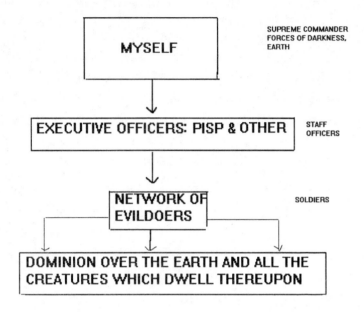

The objective to which we are all working is at the bottom.

This in turn led to a question from one of the members of the network, who had been carrying out some minor task which, if I remember rightly, involved research into the relative cost-effectiveness of sending large numbers of parcels by mail or private courier service. Would it be appropriate, she wondered, for us to call ourselves Satanists. She had been thinking about this for a good while but had been unable to come up with a definitive answer.

'On the whole,' I said, 'I would say that the answer to this question, and it is a very good and interesting question, is no. My Father is, of course, very closely involved in the operation we are running here, witness his recent message of support – He is, as I have just explained, the Fount and Origin of All Evil – and he keeps watch over us whilst we do what is, essentially, His work. Nevertheless, having said that, we are, or at least I am, a free agent. I make my own choices, identify policy, develop strategies etc with your help, but independent of My Father's direction. He communicates with me, of course, but he does not tell me what to do. I see Him, essentially, more as a resource to be called upon for information, advice, support and guidance'.

I think that everyone there assembled found this quite reassuring.

WHY NOW . . . ?

This is a question which I have been asked many times. I was asked it again that very night. 'Why, O Master,' one of the city's Members of the Scottish Parliament asked me, 'have you chosen to come among us now, at this time?'

I had to come at some point, of course, so it might as well be now. I think some of the people who ask the question are prompted by mere laziness. They would rather postpone the armageddon until a bit later, not for any real reason, but because of some deep-seated, in-built need to procrastinate over important things.

But if you want reasons, consider this. It has been almost 2000 years since the first Christ and his shambling bunch of incompetents walked the Earth. Sullied it. Fished and talked nonsense by the shores of Galilee. It's time someone else had a go. Two thousand years is a fair crack of the whip. Give the whip to someone who knows how to use it. Someone who knows how to inflict real pain with it.

You can see the signs of ripeness for my coming all around you. The whole history of the last 2000 years has been leading to this moment. You can see squalor, decay, greed, violence, corruption, filth, war and despair wherever you go. There is nothing new about this, of course. These are essential parts of the human condition. But what is new is that before, people have always been convinced that things were going to get better. Either God would deliver them, or man would make it better himself with his technology.

That's not so anymore. God is dead. Technology is a wonderful thing, but it isn't making people's lives any better any more. It makes their lives easier by eliminating tedious, dirty jobs, then it puts them out of work. It cures them of diseases, then it becomes so expensive that they can't afford it. It makes communication easier, and people find themselves increasingly isolated because they never see anyone. People have lost their faith in it. They have lost their faith.

They want me. It is My Time.

AND WHY HERE . . . ?

This question is even easier to answer. My Father, in his infinite evil wisdom, must have known it thirty and more years ago, when He caused me to be born here.

First of all, you have to think of all those blue-rinse Morningsiders, the preachers, the bankers, the lawyers. They're born to be my followers. The city's full of cant and hypocrisy, double standards, double dealing, licensed theft and dishonesty. It's my natural habitat. Edinburgh has always been like that, but it's now the centre of the universe too. It always has been, of course, at least in the minds of its inhabitants.

But things have recently become much worse. Or, from my point of view, much better. Now there is a parliament here. Edinburgh is the seat of government. It is accruing power and influence. It is full of politics and politicians. My Father, in His infinite wisdom, foresaw the 1997 general election victory of the Labour Party, and its consequences for Scotland, and the great benefit that could be derived from these. For the Purpose, I mean, for Evil. Where there is power, where there is politics, and where there are politicians, there is greed, envy, corruption, and evil. Where there is new power, there is a chance to be in at the start, to shape that greed, envy and corruption, to harness it for one's own (or one's Father's) purposes, to bend it to one's own (or ditto) ends. What better place could have been chosen for me? What better springboard to world domination and a Reign of Terror could there possibly be? I see my Father's plan for me in all its terrible majesty. I shall rise to control the new government. We shall soon declare ourselves independent, then other nations shall fall under our sway. The United Kingdom shall be united once more, though it shall be united in shackles under my black yoke. Soon thereafter the rest of the world will join it in oppression. Edinburgh will be at the centre. Think what an influence Scotland wields in the world already, and it isn't even a proper country yet. Everyone has heard of us. Everyone knows our kilts and our shortbread and our whisky and our friendly football fans. Soon, all shall be living under our terrible domination. They shall tremble at the mention of our name. Scotland, Land of the Dark Lord.

Oh aye, that'll be right. All this in Scotland?

Do you know, he was striding up and down when he was ranting just then, waving his right arm about like he was getting ready to invade Poland.

Mind you, it would be good if we were a real country again.

BEETROOT

Sometimes I put beetroot juice in my eyes. It looks like blood, so it has an excellent effect. Very dramatic. Makes the world seem a more rose-tinted spectacle.

I feel some slight warmth towards the Grocer when I remember that I am fortunate in having access to a ready and plentiful supply of these vegetables. Though it must be said that, as vegetables go, beetroot is particularly inexpensive.

THE TRUTH

I can't stand this any more. He's telling you shite. I'm going to tell you what's really going on. He never reads this stuff you know. He just spouts it out and expects me to write it down. Sometimes he looks over my shoulder to make sure I'm writing it as he tells me to, but he never reads it otherwise. I keep the book with me, so I would know if he did. From now on, if you see a bit with 'the truth' at the top of it, you'll know it's me speaking.

He's out just now. I don't know what he's doing, but

it's bound to be something that's not very nice. Maybe he's actually gone to the office. Probably gone to see a man about world domination. So I'm going to give you a bit of the truth. You haven't had any so far, so it'll be a real change for you.

We've been writing this book for ages now. Weeks. Months. He's never read a word of it. As long as I make what I'm telling you now look the same as what he tells you, it won't make any difference to him. He'll never know. I'll just write whenever I get the chance. When he's not here or when he's thinking.

Some of what he's told you is probably true. I don't know whether or not he's really the Antichrist or not but He's no Buddha, that's for sure. He's an evil bastard. That stuff about the cows, the cattle killers, I reckon that's all true. The Bag of Limbs is too. He's done millions of unsavoury things.

And he's so miserable. I've never heard him make a joke. He's never once smiled at me. He sighs all the time.

What he's told you about me is all lies. For one thing, I'm not a Grocer. I'm a greengrocer. There's a difference.

And he's not telling you the whole truth about himself. People hate him. He hates himself. You can tell.

It'll be interesting to see whether he tells you the truth about his wife.

ALL AGOG AT GOGS'S TRATTORIA

After our discussion of the structure of Evil and of my Father's message of support, I dismissed the others and told the PISP officers and a select few of the members of the network (two titled ones, a gallery owner, a BBC executive, a property developer, a senior curator at the National Museum of Scotland and someone who said she ran the Festival Fringe) that I thought a small celebration was in order, so I suggested that we go to Gordon's Trattoria on the High Street and have a meal. It would be my treat, as I felt that they had earned it.

This was a real slap-up meal – everyone was allowed to have a starter, a main course and a pudding, except the Grocer, of course, and I ordered five bottles of the house white and two of the red.

I ordered the Grocer an onion and some water.

Before the food came I delivered a small toast. I toasted the network members, though I felt it appropriate to add here that we had only just begun and there was much, much more to be done though having said that we had made an auspicious start and it was genuinely something to celebrate. We can now, I said to them, go forward secure in the knowledge that we are capable of carrying out our task and we can be confident of our ability to achieve great things.

I concluded on a personal note by toasting Meek individually, thanking her for her role in the recent success. I talked about her sterling support over the past few months, and her dedication to our cause, and I may even have said that I would be lost without her. I noticed at this point that Judith was looking distinctly put out. At the end of the evening, as Meek and I were setting out to walk back home, I realised that there had been no sign of Judith for at least three quarters of an hour, and made up my mind to have a quick word when I next saw her to see if I'd hurt her feelings.

Maybe she was just in a bad mood.

THE TRUTH

I remember that meal. He blethered on for ages. Droning on about a fine beginning and a long uphill struggle to follow. He said mighty oaks from little acorns do grow. No-one listened to him. He was spouting shite as usual. And there was an argument when someone ordered the veal. Not because it's unethical, obviously. Not even because it was the most expensive thing on the menu. I don't know much about women, but even I could tell that the argument wasn't really about the veal. What's a man like him doing with two attractive women fighting over him like that? It's ridiculous.

I had spaghetti.

He got very pissed at the end and a bit maudlin. It was his wife's favourite restaurant.

CONTINUING OUT ON A LIMB

At the next meeting of PISP it was decided that, since the Bag of Limbs initiative had been such a success, it should be adopted as an on-going and continuative strategy. Meek was appointed officer in charge with sole responsibility for limb-gathering, and it was agreed that we would try to implement Bag of Limb incidents on a schedule of one per month, preferably on the second Friday of each month, exactly midway between the two regular monthly meetings of PISP, which would allow for any special planning contingencies which might arise at the first PISP meeting of each month, and would allow media reaction to be assessed at the second.

It was also decided that it would be a good idea to commence the process of introducing at least one other strategy per month to run alongside the limbs initiative. In this way we would quickly build up a suite or portfolio of concurrent strategies all designed to dovetail neatly with each other and combine to speed the implementation process. I appointed Judith Development Officer – she was to be in charge of co-ordinating the process of generating new ideas (in addition to carrying out her duties as Press and PR Officer), though I did say that I was going to contribute to this aspect of our activities to a very high degree because I felt it incumbent on me, as the Earthly Embodiment of Evil, to generate most of the ideas and put them into effect.

It was also decided that I should go some way towards declaring myself to the world. I should not reveal myself, as yet, in All My Glory, nor should I reveal my earthly identity, but I should make it known that there was an Antichrist at large in the world, and that it was I. The first thing to do, it was decided, was that I should write a letter to the Scotsman saying that I was the Earthly Embodiment of Evil, claiming responsibility for the Bag of Limbs, and explaining my mission to achieve dominion over the Earth and all the creatures that dwell thereupon in the name of Evil.

THE TRUTH

I'm going to tell you the real story. But there's a couple of things I need to get off my chest.

See this Grocer of Doom business? I hate that. I'm a greengrocer. I've complained to him. I explained that a grocer is someone whose stock is general food stuffs and also household items such as cleaning materials and possibly small-scale hardware items. I sell fruit and vegetables – fresh produce. I always have. I've always been a greengrocer.

Now he's started calling me Turnip. Tomshie sometimes, when he wants to be couthie and Scottish. He thinks it's funny. Bastard. My name's George. George Borthwick. I hate him. Like everybody else who knows him. Everybody hates him because he's an evil bastard.

I saw him in the street the other day. He didn't see me. Offered a sweetie to this little kiddie. Says, 'Do you want this sweetie, small child?' Imagine that. Imagine calling the kiddie small child. That's no way to speak. Anyway, the kiddie says 'Yes, please' all polite, so he just laughs and smacks her in the face. 'Tough break kid,' he says. 'How very unfortunate for you.' How could he? Anyone did that to a child of mine I'd kill him.

LETTERS PAGE

My letter wasn't published, so I wrote another. This wasn't published either, so I gave up pursuing that avenue for the time being. I was, we decided, probably insufficiently well known at this point to get a letter like that published. You do get a lot of weirdos writing to the papers, and letters-page editors have to be careful.

THE TRUTH

He killed his wife, you know. Made it look like an accident. Brained her in the kitchen. Got away with it. Pretended to be heartbroken. Gave a convincing performance.

Maybe he was heartbroken. The lady who lives next door to him told me about it one day. She said, 'It's a terrible shame, you know. They were such a loving couple. Doted on each other, you know. So happy. Mr Hepton's never been the same since.'

Too right. Murdering bastard. Evil bastard. He was heartbroken, but he had to kill her. He told me all about it. Says his father wanted it that way.

MAILSHOT FROM THE DEVIL: AN EXERCISE IN DIRECT MARKETING

I decided to do a mailshot with Judith. One reason for doing this was for a bit of man-management. Woman-management, actually. She was becoming a bit distracted for some reason. I suspected her enthusiasm was waning a little, so I thought that if I got her involved in a large project under my own personal supervision I might be able to gee her up a bit.

The main reason, though, was for more publicity. If letters weren't going to get published, there was a chance of attracting attention to our cause with some more substantial mailing. We identified our target group: journalists. We wanted to attract as much attention as possible, so it was the only thing to do, to go to the people who decide where the population at large directs its attention. We made up a list by buying all the papers and watching all the television news programmes and listening to the radio bulletins for a week. We decided on 76 names. Scotland's top 76 journalists.

THE TRUTH

I've heard him at night. My room is next to his. Mine's a boxroom. No windows. His is his own proper bedroom. Nice big bed. Curtains. Fitted wardrobe.

He cries all night. Sobbing heaving crying. His eyes are red raw when I bring him his breakfast in the morning (two poached eggs on dry toast and a cup of weak milky tea). His voice is husky and cracked and he's deathly pale. White as a ghost.

He needs help.

And his breath stinks.

Guidelines on the Implementation of Evil

Defection: turning the good to Evil

1. Goodness is mere weakness.

2. It follows, therefore, that 'the good', as they like to call themselves, are easy to turn to our side.

3. The correct procedures for this are set out elsewhere, but the techniques which can be employed include: violence, distraction, cruelty, persuasion, bribery, sex, corruption, force, argument, despair, hunger, frustration, and desire. There are many others.

4. The only factor in 'the good', as they like to call themselves, which militates against our being able to turn them, is stubbornness.

5. The correct procedure for dealing with stubborn opposition is brutal extermination.

MAILSHOT DAY

Procuring the 76 Labrador puppies was not easy. It involved raids on three breeders' establishments and was reminiscent of a scene from a Walt Disney animation. Ironically, the raids themselves made the news but the news media assumed this was the work of animal liberationists, so this coverage did not benefit the cause. We should have anticipated it. A stupid mistake. We would have to beef up our press operation. Keep a closer eye on it.

The most difficult part of the plan was dreaming up 76 different ways to kill the puppies. We could, of course, have drowned them all together in half an hour, but we thought that it would make much more impact, once the story began to come out, if 76 different means of despatch were employed. People would be impressed by the dedication and imagination required. As the mailshot needed, if it were to have maximum impact, to be prepared, collated and dispatched in one day, it proved an administrative nightmare, not least in getting hold of all the necessary equipment. It took weeks of careful planning. However, I am very good at careful planning. I have had years of practice. Scotland would never have had a parliament if I had not personally supervised and overseen the necessary preparations.

On the day appointed Judith and I got to work early as there was much to be done. The house resembled a toilet-paper advertisement gone crazy. We were momentarily distracted by the antics of some of the puppies as they gambolled on the living-room carpet, but we had planned it all out in advance, and had a strict schedule to keep to with an hour-by-hour quota of puppies to deal with. We spent the first part of the morning in the kitchen, using the appliances we had assembled there: deep-frying, running through a bacon slicer (borrowed from Mr McKerracher, the friendly butcher on Leith Walk), microwaving, roasting and baking in a conventional oven, griddling, pureeing, steaming, boiling, freezing, eviscerating and so on.

We had work stations in every room in the house. We

hadn't expected the day to go without a hitch, and indeed it didn't. There are some things which you just can't plan for. Do you, for instance, have any idea how long even a tiny puppy can survive in a spin drier? Puppies of a certain age are much harder to stamp on than pigeons.

Finally we moved on to the tool shed and, by 4 o'clock that afternoon we had 76 tiny corpses (though some of them, because they were a bit runny, were in Tupperware containers) all of which had been killed in different ways, except for the extra one which had had to be sawn in half when the hover-mower had broken down. Some of them, we knew, would be difficult to identify at first as having once been a puppy, but we also knew that, once the story began to break, people would realise what they had been sent. We also anticipated the effect of our mailshot being somewhat exaggerated by this consideration – if you send a load of journalists something which marks them out as somehow special, others will claim to have been sent it as well.

We packed them in pre-addressed postal packages, loaded them into the car and drove them down to the head post office.

It cost an absolute fortune to send them. I told the woman at the counter it was an outrage. She looked at me strangely when I smiled at my witticism.

Then I messed with her head.

See what he told you about the first time we met? All that
you are a worthless piece of dung stuff? It's all shite. Not
a word of it is true. Not a word. I hate that. I hate having
to listen to it and write it down.

I felt sorry for him. When we first met I felt sorry for him.
Can you believe that? Happened like this. I've seen this man
hanging around outside the shop. Gloomy looking bastard.
I've noticed him because I think he might be scaring away
the trade. One Tuesday he comes in and asks for a pound
of beetroot and an orange. I give them to him and say
that'll be 57p. He fumbles around for ages, looking for
the right change. He's clumsy, the beetroot fall out of the
paper bag I've given him. He gets flustered. Can't find any
change. Finally he gives me a £50 note. I ask him Haven't
you got anything smaller? He shakes his head. He doesn't
say anything, but I can see tears in his eyes. I say forget it,
then. He can have the beetroot and the orange, no that's
alright pal, have them on me. He offers to go down the
road to the newsagent and get some change but I say no,
you don't have to do that, pal. If you like you can pay me
back some other time. He looks really grateful, like I've
saved his life or something. But as I say, I just felt sorry
for him.

Next day he comes back and gives me the 57p. He says
he'd like to buy me a cup of tea. Well, it's Wednesday,
half-day closing, and there's been no business all day anyway
because of the rain so I say OK, thankyou very much. We
go down the road to a cafe and he starts telling me his story.
I felt sorry for him.

It was around this time that I started getting bother at the office. A man in my position does not need bother at the office. I was told that I was taking too much time off, that I was morose when I was in the office, and that I had been acting oddly. They understood that I was under a lot of strain, they said, they had been patient with me, but I really ought to start making an effort to pull myself together.

Then they said they'd heard all sorts of strange reports about me, but that they couldn't make much sense of them. Was I engaged in some sort of weird fringe political activities, they wanted to know, because if so I was in direct contravention of the terms of my contract with them. Like any civil servant, I was expressly forbidden from involvement with any political party, or from canvassing on any issue. Was I thinking of standing for the parliament myself, now that I'd got it up and running (and they appreciated all the very hard work I'd put in). Because if I was, it wasn't allowed. I'd have to resign.

I denied any political involvement, and they accepted my word, though they looked a bit dubious.

I was furious. I kept it hidden, of course, but I was seething with rage. The cheek. I was outraged. I nearly destroyed them all then and there, but I held myself back. My job was still very useful. I resolved to make some token effort to keep up appearances. They could never know the kind of strain I'd been under. It's not easy trying to bring about the Apocalypse, you know.

The one crumb of comfort was that I knew I could count on Judith's support. I had seen to it over the past year that she had been promoted and was now my deputy. I felt reasonably sure that she would be able to keep the buggers off my back.

NEWSHOUNDS

Despite the small initial hiccough with the animal liberationist attributions, the stories in the paper were very gratifying indeed. It was something I hadn't considered properly before – it's something which is often said but I'd never thought it true – but you can actually cause more outrage with carefully orchestrated cruelty to animals than you can with many kinds of cruelty to humans.

The papers were full of it two days later, once the parcels had been delivered. The Scottish Sun screamed **FIND THIS SICKO**. The Scotsman said **Puppy Parcels Probe in Edinburgh**. One of the stories said:

> Edinburgh Police are today on the lookout for the sick pervert who creamed several young puppies and sent them through the post to top journalists, *writes Stuart Brown*. The puppies, some of them so mutilated that they had to be put into Tupperware boxes to stop them from leaking, had all been killed in different ways.
>
> Chief Inspector Gordon Allan, of Lothian and Borders Police, said 'this is absolutely sickening. How anyone could do this to young puppies, and we think they were all labradors, though we have no way of knowing, is absolutely beyond me. We will try our

utmost to catch this obviously very sick individual.
He or she obviously needs help.'

Which just goes to show how much the police know
about anything.

The note I'd enclosed in my puppy parcels had said,
'Behold ye and tremble for He is coming and He is the
Beast. It'll get worse, you know', and it only took a few
days for some bright spark at the Herald to make the
connection between the parcels and the Bag of Limbs.
Now, at last, and for the first time, I was being referred
to as evil in public. It was the first step down the road to
acceptance as the antichrist.

Long road, though.

THE TRUTH

So we go into this cafe and get our teas. He pays. He
asks whether I would like a cake or an iced bun and
I say no, just the tea will be fine thankyou. So we sit
down. He stirs five sugars into his tea and then he tells
me he's cursed.

I know what you mean, I say.

No, he says, you don't understand.

Yes, I say, I do.

No, he says, you don't understand. You can't possibly
understand. And then he gets this look in his eyes. It's very
strange. I go all cold. Shivers down my back. I listen.

I am evil, he tells me.

I'm not very nice myself, I say.

No, he says, you don't understand. I am evil. I *am* evil. Evil is me. We are one and the same thing.

Then he slurps his tea while it's still too hot and spills some. He sighs. He's got tea stains on his shirt.

WORKING CLASS PEOPLE

The network was growing. Meek was recruiting any number of professional persons. A sort of officer class. Judith, because of the nature of her activities, was recruiting a lot of grunts. Footsoldiers.

The people who were coming to her outreach classes really were the most appalling bunch, with their lank hair and nylon clothes. I had to meet them occasionally, but I could barely bring myself to talk to them. I'd had very little to do with the Edinburgh proletariat. One had passed them in the street, of course, and spoken to the ones who worked behind counters in shops and so on, but it was never very pleasant.

I don't think Judith cared very much for them, either.

THE WAYS IN WHICH EVIL IS
COMMUNICATED TO ME

Being the embodiment of Evil, I am very aware of Evil's ways. This means that My Father can communicate with me using many different media. As it happens, many of them are transport-related. For instance, sometimes My Father communicates with me using traffic lights. He uses a code to convey an Impression, so that, when I am driving along, I know that if I encounter three red lights in a row, He is being, generally, negative, whereas if I see three green lights, he is feeling positive. He often uses the code when I have a question to ask him, in which case the three red lights translate as 'no', and the three greens as 'yes'.

We have a walking code as well. When I am walking along the road, He communicates with me by sending cars and lorries. If, say, three cars pass me by the time I reach a certain point, I know that he intends such and such a thing, but if none pass, I know that His Intentions are otherwise. I don't want to go into too much detail in case my messages are intercepted, so I won't tell you any more, but I did think it important to establish the fact that I am in direct and constant communication with My Father.

Guidelines on the Implementation of Evil

Transport

The mutual influence of Evil and the transport infrastructure can scarcely be overestimated. There are a number of factors at work:

1. When placed in control of an automobile the majority of members of the public lose sight of and contact with the social factors which would otherwise inhibit their natural tendency to Evil. This trend, according to our studies, is particularly marked in Los Angeles, but can be seen in any major city.

2. By generating further mayhem, chaos and disorder on the

roads, we can exacerbate this trend. The key to this is planning and bureaucracy (see previous guidelines).

3. Ditto public transport, though in a slightly different way.

THE TRUTH

He's actually decided to go to work today, so I can tell you a bit more. It'll be easy to hide it from him when he gets back. He'll be in an even worse mood than usual because his work's not going that well, so he'll sit quiet for an hour or two and then start talking without looking at me and just expect me to write down what he's saying.

He never looks at this precious book of his, and it's all in my writing anyway, so he won't be able to tell what I'm up to even if he looks over my shoulder.

Right, he's spilled his tea and he starts sighing. He looks really miserable so I feel sorry for him even more than I did before. For about five minutes he looks as if he's about to say something. Then he finally summons up the courage to speak.

'I am the Antichrist', he says. I ask him why. How he knows, how can he be sure? but the funny thing is, I already believe him. There is something very odd about him. I feel sorry for him. He tells me all about the signs, tells me he's done some very bad things. Much the same stuff as he's been making me write down. I ask him what he can have done that is so terrible, but he won't say. He just starts crying into his cup of tea and says he doesn't want to be evil, he just wants to be normal. Says all he ever wanted was a nice house, a secure job, a good wife and a family but this is not going to be possible. Then he puts his tea down and pushes it away and says, 'Take this cup away from me for I don't want to taste its poison.' I say that's from Jesus Christ Superstar isn't it, I went to see it with Mrs Findlay when it was on at the Playhouse and she bought the record so I recognise it. He doesn't say anything for a while. Then he says again that he just wants to be normal. I can see that he isn't normal, so I don't bother telling him that he is. It's obviously not true.

Instead I say to him, 'Come on, I'll take you home. Where do you live?' He's in a bit of a state, and it's ages before he can tell me, but he finally does and I start to walk him there. It's about a mile, but it takes us about 40 minutes to get there. He's leaning on me, I'm propping him up. People passing us think he's pissed or that we're a pair of old poofs.

We get to his house and he sits down at the kitchen table, his head in his hands. The place is a disgusting mess. Absolute tip. Dirty dishes everywhere. Filth on everything, piles of rotting food. I say, 'Jesus how can you live like this?' and he says, 'I can't.' I ask him when he last ate and he says he can't remember. There are some half-eaten fishfingers and baked beans on a plate near the sink and they look as if they've been there for no more than a week. Everything else looks pre-historic. I tell him he's got to look after himself. I scour the place for something edible and I find some leeks, carrots, turnip and potatoes and a jar of Bovril. I boil these up for an hour and make some soup. While I'm doing this I find a couple of bowls and scrape them out then wash them, then I make a start on cleaning his kitchen. I've made hardly any impression on all the filth by the time the soup's ready.

I serve up the soup – he's got a disgusting way of slurping it. Practically inhales it. It's far worse than the noise he makes drinking tea. I think he's grateful. He doesn't say anything, he still looks miserable, but he's stopped crying.

Then he points to the end of the kitchen. There are these shelves with a load of boxes and packets and tins on them. I look at the end of the second shelf down and see pasta, porridge oats, dried peas, split yellow peas, and some pearl barley which I hadn't noticed earlier but would have been useful for thickening the soup. Very neatly stacked. There's several tins – of fruit and of baked beans, spaghetti and ravioli in tomato sauce. I notice that they're all in alphabetical order. 'That's where it happened,' he says. 'What happened?' I ask. 'Under that shelf,' he says. 'What?' I ask, but he doesn't say anything. He's starting to look miserable again so I drop the subject.

About an hour later I make us another cup of tea. We drink it. He looks a bit more cheerful now. I say I must be heading off back home to my room and he looks a bit put out for a minute, but then he nods and says, 'Yes, I suppose,' and then he sighs. I put on my coat and my hat and, just as I'm leaving he says to me, very quietly, 'Thank you for being so kind to me.' I say 'och, that's alright, I didn't do anything very much.' He says, 'No, really, you've been very kind, you've been a big help. I've been very low and you listen. You're a good listener. Look,' he says, 'will you come again? Come for your tea next Wednesday, will you?' 'Okidoki,' says I. 'Good,' he says. 'I'll get some sausages.'

Nobody called anybody a worthless piece of dung.

I noticed, after about three months, that although we had made a huge splash with the puppies, public interest in the continuing Bag (or Box) of Limbs Strategy (BOLS, as it was known by PISP members) was waning. We were no longer making the front pages with it. Indeed, on the fourth occasion, we only merited a 'news in brief' snippet in one of the quality dailies to the effect that 'another bag containing human body parts has been found in Edinburgh'.

This brought home to us the importance of novelty in attracting and maintaining people's interest in this type of activity.

Had we thought about it beforehand, of course, we would have realised that novelty was everything. We had all seen the news coverage of Northern Ireland, Yugoslavia, famines in Africa and so on start off big then dwindle to nothing. We would have to beef up our press and media relations operation.

That's why I was pinning all my hopes on the puppies thing, why I was determined not to late it pale away into insignificance. I would have to find some way of building on it, changing it, keeping it running with variations so as not to let it die. It was very hard work.

The strain was beginning to make me feel rather depressed. It's really hard sustaining that kind of effort. Meek was beginning to look a bit haggard too. Lumpy. She had spots and greasy hair, so I suggested that she get a few early nights, take it easy for a while. I must say that I didn't expect her to react quite like that, given that I was speaking only from a concern for her own best interests.

She looked quite miffed when I suggested it, and positively fuming when Judith chipped in with 'yes, dear, don't you think you've been overdoing it – you look very . . . tired'. There was nearly a fight.

Talk about hard work.

I told Meek it was hard enough being the antichrist without her melodramatics. I was under a lot of strain, I told her, what with work, my own personal development in Evil to accomplish and the Reign of Terror to start, and it wasn't fair of her to start these histrionics. Maybe she could put some of her energy into coming up with an idea to replace the Bag of Limbs thing, since that seemed to have died a death now. We really didn't seem to be getting anywhere, except for the puppies thing, and there were moments when even that seemed so insignificant. I should have been ruling the earth in my Father's name, but I was messing about with a bunch of upper-middle class twerps with tunnel vision, two girls and a subhuman shopkeeper. I wasn't achieving anything and I didn't know why.

We were all a bit tired and run-down.

Still. I had to keep myself from getting disillusioned. Kept telling myself mighty oaks from tiny acorns. Mighty oaks from tiny acorns. It was taking a hell of a long time, though.

THE TRUTH

Well, we sort of fell into the habit of meeting on Wednesdays. Usually I went around to his house for my tea, but sometimes he would come around to the shop to call for me and we'd go to a cafe and have tea, sausage rolls and cakes. He always paid whenever we did that. He never seemed to be short of cash, and you could tell from his house that he wasn't short of a few bob. I never really understood what he does for a living though. He would just say he worked in administration at the Scottish Office. I asked him once what does that mean? but he couldn't explain it to me. He said he'd spent a long time working on the new parliament but it was all done now and there was no excitement left in it any more. He was just running it, so it was all very boring now. He said that that's what would happen to everybody once the excitement of having a new parliament wore off – they'd get bored with it and, what was his word, cynical, that's it.

He was really miserable. He came to rely on me for company. It's strange, isn't it? He knows practically the whole of Edinburgh, the people of quality, anyway, but he was lonely.

It's the first time anyone's ever relied on me like that. I'm not very good at telling this. I've never written anything down before, except the accounts at the shop. This is a really complicated story, and I don't really understand what happened next, but I've got to try to set the record straight. He's telling you lies, and he's leaving things out, which is worse.

I couldn't let myself get disillusioned. I had to look on the bright side. Really, the puppies thing went much better than I could ever have expected. It was, at that point, the one happy thing in my life. I was very pleased with Judith, and we began to spend more time together. She still seemed a bit distant, but I was glad she'd overcome her previous lethargy and disenchantment.

The stories ran and ran, and the television coverage was both lengthy and in-depth. Which was a bit of a shame as they had very little to go on.

The police had traced the parcels to the Edinburgh post-office where I mailed them, and had spoken to the woman who took them over the counter. She, however, was totally unable to provide them with a description of the perpetrator. This was because I had blanked my image out of her mind using my powers when I did the mailing. I looked at her just after I had unburdened myself of my opinion of current postal rates, and I searched for her memory of me in her head, and I erased it. This is easy when you know how.

When the police came to interview her, all she had in her head where I had been was an empty space. They thought this was suspicious, and arrested her on suspicion of having been closely involved in the 'atrocity', or so the TV news said, but they had to let her go after a day or two. Poor cow. Everyone knew she'd been arrested. Everyone thought she was guilty, because she'd been named by the TV news. Mrs Muriel Dunblane, of 13 Haymarket Terrace, Edinburgh, who works as a clerk at the head post office in the St James Centre, Edinburgh. Poor cow.

There are some parts of My True Nature, of my role as the Earthly Embodiment of Evil, that I really enjoy.

It's a bit of a fag the rest of the time, though.

Guidelines on the Implementation of Evil

Sexism and racism

1 Sexism poses a real dilemma for the practitioner of Evil. Being, in and of itself, an Evil, one might assume that it would be worthy of serious consideration as a strategy for immediate implementation.

2. However, there are serious operational issues raised by this. Many of the most effective practitioners of Evil are the very people who would be excluded by a recruitment policy which operated on sexist principles.

3. Great care must therefore be taken not to exclude those potential practitioners who would be disadvantaged by the operation of a sexist recruitment policy, as this would work to the detriment of the network of evil-doers and therefore to the detriment of Evil itself. This is an example of the concept of self-damaging Evil at work.

4. The instances where sexism might be usefully employed might be characterised thus: where it would cause maximum annoyance to outsiders, but little or (preferably) no inconvenience to the network.

5. Ditto racism, though in a slightly different way.

THE TRUTH

What happened next is hard to explain. After a few weeks of meeting him first of all just on Wednesdays, then on Wednesdays and Sundays, then on Wednesdays, Sundays and Mondays, I noticed that I couldn't escape from him. I couldn't say no. He could make me do things. I fell under his spell, or into his clutches, I don't know which.

He made me do things. At first it was just going to the shops and bringing him food. Fish suppers and whisky. But then, one night when I'd brought him back a single pie and curry sauce, he made me cut the legs off this little white rat with a knife and fork while he ate his pie. I couldn't say no. I felt sick. He told me later it was just some kid's pet that he'd stolen earlier in the day.

What a bastard. I found myself spending more and more time with him. I couldn't help it.

PRICK

This Stuart Brown character fancied himself as a real investigative type of reporter. I don't know what was motivating him, but he was obviously trying to make his name or something because he latched on to the story like a terrier and wouldn't let go. He became quite a thorn in my flesh. Maybe more of a prick than a thorn.

He wrote about it every day. This wasn't easy because he didn't know anything, but he constantly ran stories in which he'd interviewed priests about the 'Satanic' messages found in the puppy parcels. He ran puppy-count stories – as we'd predicted, the count soon ran well over the number we'd dispatched as media figures became desperate not to be left out.

Anyway, the constant attention, wearing and at times not a little irksome though it was, was very much the sort of thing we were after as PISP strategy. We decided, though, that we would have to keep an eye on individual members of the press to make sure they didn't find out more than we intended until such time as we intended them to find it out, if you follow me.

Here's an example of the sort of thing Brown was writing. As you can see, it's pretty short on detail, but then, a lot of things you read in newspapers are.

Police are still baffled by the horrific events of last week when upwards of ninety young puppies, many of them mutilated beyond recognition, were despatched to prominent members of the media by parcel.

Meanwhile, top psychologist Dr Mary Livesey has supplied police with a breakdown of the character she thinks may be responsible for the outrage and another last month when a bag, containing human remains, was left outside a children's playground in Edinburgh.

In an exclusive interview for this paper, Dr Livesey said that the individual the police were looking for was probably motivated by a deep-seated hatred of humanity. 'The man, for I'm sure it is a

man, is obviously deeply disturbed,' she said. 'He has a number of severely anti-social tendencies, is probably a bit of a loner, and is capable of almost fanatical attention to detail.

'He obviously chose puppies because they are cute,' she said, 'and he wanted to do something terrible, something very shocking indeed.'

She has, she said, come across similar instances in the past, though this incident was quite literally 'breathtaking'.

'This sort of behaviour,' she said, 'is not uncommon in certain sorts of mental illness, though it is rarely taken to this extent. The degree of organisation this individual has shown in posting all these parcels on the same day is really quite literally breathtaking. We are clearly talking about a very disturbed, and quite possible very dangerous, individual.'

She went on to say that there is a possibility that the individual concerned was acting out some event from childhood when he or she had been frightened by a dog.

She was quite wrong about most of this, of course, but I found what she had to say quite flattering.

In any case, the inaccuracy of her remarks was irrelevant. They say that there's no such thing as bad publicity, and, for once, they are right.

THERE'S PSYCHOLOGY FOR YOU

I've come across a number of psychologists in my time, and they're all crazy. And incompetent. Meek, who has come across, and been come across by, many more, will bear witness to this.

One of the giveaways is this psychological profile business. They're always so completely wide of the mark. I'm strictly an amateur, of course, but I've seen it done. I've had it done to me. If I were to do a profile of myself, this is how it would go.

This man is obviously extremely powerful. He is possessed of a fearsomely ordered mind and a powerful intellect. He has enormous sexual drive, and no regard whatsoever for the common mass of humanity, whom he sees, with justification, as vastly inferior to himself. He will one day destroy civilisation as we know it. He will one day have the entire city of Edinburgh in his pocket.

In terms of pinpoint accuracy and succinctness, the

so-called *Dr* Livesey would never have come close to the brilliance of my own analysis. I could show her a thing or two.

BEING A BIT MORE HONEST

Maybe I flattered myself too much with that profile. I have to be honest with myself, or I shall never get it together and get to where I am supposed to be going, if you follow me. If I am doing a profile, I should include the bad things as well. Not the Evil, the bad. There's a difference.

So: Resents boring job. Resents fact that is good at boring job and has gift for administration. Resents fact that gift for administration has been carried over into his being Embodiment of Evil. Feeling a certain degree of frustration: wants to dominate entire world, knows is not succeeding, but doesn't know why. Desperately wants something to *happen*.

I spoke to Meek about my feelings. She was feeling much better. We had a good long chat. She said it was understandable that I should feel depressed every now and again. I had a long hard road to travel and I was only just setting out. I would just have to apply myself and get on with it. No-one had said it was going to be easy. There would be no help, and no-one would understand what I was going through.

No-one except her. She understands me.

I really have been most perspicacious in my choice of lieutenants. Judith is so competent and efficient. Meek is so sympathetic. They are such boons to me. I don't know what I would do without them.

THE TRUTH

As I said, I found myself spending more and more time with him. Then I found that I'd moved in to his house. It happened in a kind of blur, and I can't remember that much about it. I've got this small boxroom next to his bedroom. Gave up my room at Mrs Findlay's.

I can remember a little bit about the way he got me to move in with him, but not much. No details. Maybe he's messed with my head like he did to that Post Office woman.

I think me moving in was what he'd wanted all along. He said he liked my company, and he had a spare room. Several in fact. I wouldn't have to pay rent, he said. The thought of the 15 quid a week I could save was very tempting, so I accepted. I suppose I must have moved my things out. I don't remember doing this. I do remember that Mrs Findlay looked a bit put out when I said I was leaving. 'Just like that', she said, 'after twelve years, you're leaving. And I'd been hoping . . .' but she didn't say what.

LOWER CLASS

I was feeling a bit more buoyant, having been soothed by Meek, but my gloom returned as soon as was on my own. I was down, but at least I had, thanks to her encouragement, resolved to kick my life into gear and get it moving. So, when Judith asked me if I would be kind enough to come along to one of her outreach classes and address the people there as she was having difficulties with this particular class, I said yes. I wanted to get all these niggling little problems sorted out.

Judith said she thought it would be good for me to meet the troops and get in touch with the grass roots of the organisation. She said it would give me a different perspective from the rather rarefied and insular one I got from hanging around at the Scottish Office and from associating with the members of the network. It would give me an insight into what she called the 'real world'. She also thought it might have more impact and boost recruitment if I were to be personally involved.

I went along with her to Moray House on Holyrood Road, practically next-door to the parliament building, so I felt like I was nearly on home ground. That night's class was on the Heptonic Path to Self-fulfilment. I have to say that my heart sank when I entered the classroom. There were about fifteen people there. From what I could gather from the introductions Judith made, all the women were called Alison or Julie. There were two men. One called Ian and one called Davie. They were the ugliest, most ill-dressed and unprepossessing people I had ever met. Remember when I say this that I work in the public sector, and you get some idea of the horror I felt that evening.

Judith stood in front of them and said, 'We are very lucky to have with us tonight the founder of our movement, Mr Hector Hepton. Hector very rarely makes appearances in public, but tonight he's going to speak to us in person.'

I have to admit that this came as something of a shock. I had agreed to attend, not to speak. I looked daggers at Judith, and she motioned for me to get on with it. I spoke for ten or twelve minutes. I didn't have a clue what I was talking about. I dimly remembered some things I'd read about self-possession, calmness, inner serenity and moral soundness in a leaflet I'd once been given by a shaven headed individual in orange robes banging a drum in Princes Street. I regurgitated that, though my delivery was not very polished.

I brought my monologue to some sort of a conclusion and sat down, heavily. Judith stood up and said, 'Thankyou, Hector. I'm sure that Hector would now be delighted to answer any of your questions. Is there anything you would like to ask him?'

There was a silence which lasted for upwards of two minutes during which the class shifted uncomfortably in its chairs and turned its sullen, moronic faces to look at its cheap shoes many of which, I couldn't help but notice, where white – you know, those trainer things these people wear. Finally, one of the women raised her hand and said, 'What is the path to self-fulfilment?' I really felt like saying I had no idea, that it was just something Judith had made up, but I thought better of it so I made up some more things about inner strength and being focused inwards that I remembered from an article on Eastern philosophy I'd read in my wife's *Cosmopolitan*. Everybody sat there in silence as I spoke, and no-one volunteered another question.

When the class wound up, twenty minutes later, I said to Judith that if that bunch of numbskulls she had just shown me was the real world I wanted nothing to do with it. I upbraided her for not warning me that she was going to ask me to speak to them. Then I asked her, 'Is that all that goes on at these classes of yours? How do you manage to recruit anyone?' She said that it was usually quite lively at her classes because *she* made it interesting for them. She said it was usually entertaining for them because *she* prepared her classes in advance and didn't just stand there spouting obvious rubbish. *She* got them hooked by telling them something interesting. This group, she admitted, were particularly quiet, which was why she had asked me to come along. She'd thought that I might be able to gee them up a bit. She added a 'Ha!' Then she said, 'But you didn't make any effort whatsoever. I work very hard for you, Hector, and this is the value you put on me and my work. Nothing.'

I tried to reassure her, say that this wasn't true, but she stomped off into the night.

I was a little put out myself.

MY RAIMENT

Let me tell you about my raiment, for it will enable you to understand me that little bit more clearly. I always thought it would have been good to know a bit more about Jesus's clothes – what colour of robe he wore, whether he favoured jockey shorts or boxers or indeed an exotic thong or posing pouch – that sort of thing. The clothes maketh the man.

In the old days, my wife always used to choose my clothes for me. She would lay them out on a chair in the dressing room the night before. The only time I ever chose my own clothes was when I was a student, and I looked a complete mess.

To save myself the bother of having to decide what to wear, I always wear the same things. Obviously, some of the individual garments come and go, but they are always of the same sort and appearance.

My raiment is a clue to my identity, and, because my identity never changes, neither does my raiment. Each item of my wardrobe is invested with a special significance of its own when I put it on. Each item represents some aspect of my Power.

The grey pin-stripe suit is the perfect wrapping for my grey, bloodless, stony heart. I have fifteen of these suits, virtually identical, made for me by a bespoke tailor in the New Town. Each suit, when worn by me, consists of The Jacket of Disorder, the Trousers of Torment, and the Waistcoat of World Domination. The waistcoats have convenient ticket pockets, where I can keep my Lothian Region Travelcard, which enables me to travel about the city in the furtherance of Evil for really only a nominal monthly outlay.

The Striped Shirt of Civility represents my outward conformity with social and cultural norms: any human interaction depends upon these, at first. A striped shirt is a clear sign of conformity. It signals a lack of danger. It is the mark of the humdrum. I wear it as a kind of snare, to lure people to me by my apparent (but not real) ordinariness. I buy my shirts at C&A. My wife used to go to Jenners' for them, but C&A shirts are just as good.

The Bow Tie of Urbanity (which is red with a white polka dot) represents a raffish quality which some people respond to. It signals my wit and sophistication, but also gives some subtle hint of the dangers which lie beneath my surface.

The Black Brogues of Boundless Despair are perfect

for stamping on the faces of those who would stand in my way.

The Purple Socks of Sarcasm are a clear indication, for those who have eyes to see, that all is not what it seems.

Guidelines on the Implementation of Evil

Right and Wrong

1. The question of morality might, at first sight, seem a hard one for the practitioner of Evil to come to terms with. However, this is not the case.

2. Consider all the usual examples: murders, rapes, swindled pensioners, beatings, etc. It is easy to see how these fit the moral criteria which society establishes as determining wrong-doing.

3. It is possible to construct alternative sets of criteria, according to which these actions are no longer classified as wrong-doing.

4. However, it is far more effective simply to reject all such criteria – or at least the relevance of all such criteria – out of hand. To put it another way, the response of the seasoned practitioner of Evil to such an incident would be to say, 'I know why this incident is wrong, but I don't care.'

5. Exercise
   There is not necessarily a total identification along the following lines
   good = right; Evil = wrong.

You might also like to consider the following statements:

a. What this country needs is a good kick up the arse: austerity, cutbacks, no public spending. That'll get it back on its feet.

b. There are too many people in Africa, that's why they're starving. Let them.

Both of these statements are Evil. But are they wrong?

THE TRUTH

I wish I'd not left Mrs Findlay's. I didn't mind her. She said too much sometimes. She was not what you would call a handsome woman. But we were the same age and we had the same tastes. Sometimes we used to sit together in her front room and listen to golden oldies, Russ Conway. She used to say it was a wonder that a fine man like me had never married. Made me feel good to hear someone say that. She said I reminded her sometimes of her late husband William. I had many of his fine qualities. Upright. Well respected. Honest. Careful with money.

FOLLOWING THE PUPPIES LEAD

The hunt for the Puppies Sicko, now recognised as the individual who was also responsible for the Bag of Limbs outrage (on account of the accompanying notes having been shown to have been run out on the same electronic typewriter), continued but got nowhere. No-one had any leads to go on. There came a day when only this Stuart Brown was writing about me any more, and not very well at that. All he was able to say was that police were still looking for the individual who had carried out the 'atrocity'. They had enlisted the aid of a psychic.

I didn't think that this was the sort of coverage we deserved, so I decided to do it again. I could not allow myself to fade from the public domain.

This time, as a tribute to Torquil, I decided on kittens. Because I felt, rightly as it turned out, that I didn't have to make as much effort as I had with the labradors in order to generate a great deal of publicity (and because of considerations of time and the availability of resources) I decided to deep-fry them.

I took the unusual and highly irregular step of not waiting for the next meeting of the PISP group to inform them of this decision and have it discussed and refined, informing the various members by telephone instead. Time was of the essence.

The operation was simplicity itself. At 2 A.M., I packed the 76 kittens (easily obtained from Cat Protection people) into 10 boxes, loaded them into the back of a van I'd hired the day before from Vincent's Van Go and drove to a small town in West Lothian. I broke into the Marinara Fish 'n' Chick Bar on the High Street, and, at approximately 3 A.M., turned on the deep-fryers. I waited until the oil reached the requisite temperature, then poured the kittens from the boxes and into the fryers. It was quite difficult to get them all done to the same degree, and I have to admit that one or two of them were rather blackened and crispy, but I don't think this was desperately important.

The mailing the next morning was simply a matter of repeating the labrador process. I tried to make sure that it was Mrs Muriel Dunblane who processed the parcels, but it transpired that she had been transferred to other duties. Handing over the parcels to the woman who was behind the counter, I took the precaution once more of erasing her memory of me. This time, though, in a brilliant flash of inspiration, I decided to replace the memory with the image of a large fish, a sea-bass as it happens, in a purple shirt. She would later, if (or rather when) she was questioned by the police, be completely unable to avoid revealing her memory of this image to them.

This made me chuckle.

EXERCISE

Thanks to Judith and Meek, the network of Evil-doers was growing. I had decided to leave all the details of recruitment to them, but I thought it might be an idea to conduct an exercise, much as the Army holds manoeuvres. There were two reasons for this: first, it would give the members of the network a chance to practise their skills on my behalf, second, it would give me a chance to see how effective we were as an operation.

A number of logistical difficulties presented themselves. Paramount amongst these was the concern to do something which would be significant but which, since this was only an exercise and we had not prepared as yet to assume full dominion over the Earth and all the creatures that dwell thereupon, would not attract the attention of the Earthly authorities. Another concern was that, since the majority of the members of the network recruited by Judith, the footsoldiers (and therefore the people going out to do the actual legwork) were working class, (if the sort of people I had met at Judith's class were anything to go by) the activity to be undertaken had to be menial in nature, and certainly couldn't involve any brainpower.

I devised the following plan. Its beauty was that its end, though in itself a fairly trivial one, would nevertheless have a deeply unsettling effect on certain people. Especially those rich or stupid enough to live in villages.

The plan was this: Members of the network were to disperse to all points, and begin a programme of defacement of village boundary signs. Specifically, those boundary signs which said 'X welcomes you, please drive slowly' were to be amended (with a knife, or similar implement) to read 'X welcomes you, please d i e slowly'. Chillingly amusing, I thought.

Plus, of course, those signs which read 'please drive carefully' would be amended to 'please d i e carefully'. A lovely image: don't get shit on the carpet. Make sure you empty your bladder. Have you made a will?

Right. We haven't done any guidelines for a while. There's a lot more to get through, so we'd better do some more now.

Guidelines on the Implementation of Evil

Cruelty

Cruelty is, of course, a necessary concomitant of Evil. Put simply, the position is that you can have cruelty without Evil, but you cannot have Evil without cruelty.

Viewed another way, cruelty can be seen as simply an Aspect of Evil, rather than as a thing or a quality in its own right. In neither case, however, can cruelty, from the point of view of the Practitioner of Evil, be seen as in any way unnecessary. (The cliché 'unnecessary cruelty' is widely current in public discourse and the media, but is not applicable to Practitioners – they must be cruel to be Practitioners. This might be summed up thus: you've got to be cruel to be our kind.)

The following are some of the more popular forms of cruelty. They are rated for effectiveness on a scale from 1 to 11.

Physical cruelty: one of the most common forms. There are many varieties of physical cruelty, including torture. In most cases, especially as a means of subjugating, humiliating or destroying individuals, or as a means of individual torment, it is highly effective. Rating 9.3

Emotional cruelty: this is sometimes hard to distinguish from mental cruelty (see below), which reflects the current position amongst Practitioners that the emotional/mental distinction commonly made by the populace at large is a false one, or is at least by no means as clear cut as is popularly assumed. The main use of emotional cruelty is the targeting and driving to distraction (q.v.) of specific individuals within certain sorts of inter-personal relationship characterised by a high degree of emotional commitment on the part of the targetee. In these cases it is highly effective, rating 8.7 though, because of its limited application, it rarely achieves this high degree of efficacy in practice.

Mental cruelty: the term mental cruelty is often used simply as a sort of dustbin term for any sort of cruelty not characterised by physical violence. The correct term for this, however, is non-physical cruelty (see below). Mental cruelty is often hard to distinguish from emotional cruelty (see above), the main differences being the absence of any degree of emotional commitment on the part of the targetee, and the high degree of usage of such devices as suggestion, threat, insinuation etc. Because of the absence of emotional commitment on the part of the targetee, it tends to be less effective when employed against specific individuals, rating 7.9. However, research is under way within this network into methods of adapting mental cruelty for broadcast purposes.

Non-physical cruelty: this is a kind of dustbin term for any sorts of cruelty which are not physical and cannot be characterised as either emotional or mental. As such it does not have an effectiveness rating.

THE TRUTH

I cannot say no to him. It's impossible. I just do whatever he asks me. It disgusts me. He disgusts me. I disgust myself. But I can't help it. He has this power over me. It's his eyes, maybe. It's like I'm falling into a deep dark hole, being drawn into it against my will. I'm too weak. Maybe I'm more like a rabbit caught in the glare of headlights. I don't like it. He's made me do some terrible things. He gives me no choice.

I'm a slave. I cater to his every whim. He treats me like dirt. I bring him his breakfast every morning. I cook him soup. I bring him vegetables. Flowers too, if I have them in the shop. Never a word of thanks. Never any kind word.

It was never like this at Mrs Findlay's.

Bastard.

CACKLE

I was still laughing when I came back from the post office having posted the kittens. I sat at the kitchen table and cackled into a cup of tea for about half an hour. Suddenly, I became aware of a Presence. I looked up and saw Torquil. I told him what I'd done and he said, 'Very nice, Very nice. Your Father will be proud.'

Still chuckling, I told him about the fish-image. He had an idea.

'Look,' he said. 'You can do this with your mind, you can erase thoughts, you can make people think things. Why not do it bigger? Why not put something in everyone's mind? Everyone's got a mind, most of them anyway. They got a mind, you can put something there. Something bad, maybe.'

I was very excited about this. 'What a great idea,' I said. 'Excellent idea. But what? What should I make people think?'

'How should I know?' he said. 'What do I know about

Evil? I'm just a messenger. You're the Antichrist, Evil's your department. You'll think of something.'

'OK,' I said. 'I'll think of something. But there's another problem.'

'Problems, problems,' he interrupted, 'with you it's always problems. What now?'

'Well,' I said, 'I've never put thoughts into more than one mind at any time. I don't know how to do it all at once, to loads of people, to everybody. How do you do that?'

'Again', he said, 'how should I know? You're the Evil One, you figure it out.'

So saying he shrugged his shoulders and disappeared in a ginger huff.

I decided that the best way to work it out would be to start small and work my way up to the full thing. Practice. Practice makes perfect. It would be worth the effort. This sort of control over what people are thinking would be a very useful tool for controlling the crawling, slimy, snivelling mass of humanity once I assumed dominion over all the Earth and the creatures that dwell thereupon.

THE TRUTH

He told me all this stuff about himself. I've told some of it to you. About how he was so sad. How he was evil, and all the terrible things he'd done. Well, you know how it is when you're having a heart-to-heart with someone. You're listening, and they're spilling their guts out to you. You listen for a while, a good long while maybe. But sooner or later you start telling them things about yourself.

You have to. You can't help it. They can be very private things too. Things you've never told anybody else. Things you'd never tell your mother or your best friend. Things you maybe didn't realise were true until you said them. Or wouldn't admit to yourself.

Well, I'd been listening to him for ages. He'd been telling me all this stuff about himself. I don't know now how much of it was true, but I know that what he said about his wife was, and about the terrible things he's done, even though a lot of what he's made me write in this book is pure plain shite. One evening, though, he starts telling me I'm a good listener. 'How did you get that way?' he asks me. 'You're so patient, such a good listener,' he says. 'That usually only comes with great suffering. Believe me I know.' And then he looks at me all expectantly.

It was a lure. A trick. He wanted me to tell him things about myself.

I fell for it. I wish I hadn't.

A LOT ON OUR PLATES

At the next meeting of the PISP group there was a great deal to be discussed. First we had to identify messages to be broadcast to the entire population. This, it was agreed, was probably the most important task facing us. Then, we had to have progress reports from our network of agents in the field on reaction, as it continued, to our various operations and strategies, including the Bag of Limbs and the twin animal-remains mailshots. Then we had to devise a strategy for dealing with any member of the press who might, perhaps accidentally, get too close to us with the attendant risk of premature exposure. Finally, we had to devise, in accordance with a previous decision of the PISP group, a strategy to run alongside those which had already been implemented.

Because there was a lot to get through, I suggested that discussion be kept to a minimum and that any questions or points of order which arose be kept until the end of the meeting to facilitate our dealing with all the matters in hand in a speedy and efficient manner. I had specifically instructed the Grocer to note only the salient points. Perhaps the ignorant arse doesn't know what salient means. Thinks it's something to do with salt. Since the minutes are so complex, I'll just present the salient points now and, having done that, I'll see if any further elaboration is required at the end.

Of course I know what salient means. If what you're saying is all shite, though, how am I supposed to know which bit is most important?

Come on Turnip-features, you can't still be writing, unless you're even more stupid and worthless than we thought.

Yes, that last bit too. Why not? Let everyone know what a dilatory, shambling, useless piece of dung you are.

Ready? Right.

There were, if you remember, four main topics on the agenda. Let's deal with them each in turn. Put a little number in the left margin as we start each one. One.

1. Identification of messages for broadcast purposes

It was decided, after extensive discussion, that we should

start small. The first idea to be put into people's heads should be 'I don't feel very well'. This would lead to a general negatory emotional state (gloom/depression). PISP group members, together with our extensive network of agents in the field, would monitor the effectiveness of this stratagem. If the stratagem proved to be effective, the next message to be broadcast would be stronger in content i.e. 'the Universe is a bleak and barren place devoid of any meaning or significance and I am completely alone in it'. Subsequent messages would be identified at a later date, but, at the appropriate moment, it would obviously be very useful if some sort of political discontentment could be fostered by this means. Dissatisfaction with the current political situation could be encouraged. A suitably subtle suggestion that what was needed was a complete overthrowing of the machinery of government and its replacement by a single leader with a background in administration might be all that was needed to carry me to power on a wave of popular feeling that I could then harness to my own ends. Obviously. However, this was a long way off, and I needed to practise first. I'd also need to be very careful about timing, because if I tried too early and wasn't at the peak of my powers I might not be able to bring it off properly. On the other hand, wait too long and power could be usurped by others, and who knows how difficult it might then be to wrest control. I might even have to start all over again. Tricky.

2. Reaction to strategies previous and continuing
A selection of newspaper reports and video-taped television news bulletins were presented for examination by PISP group members. The results were generally held to be most encouraging. News reports were beginning to concentrate

on a growing tide of Evil spreading through the land, and moral decay and spiritual malaise were themes running throughout the commentary. On the negative side, one or two commentators in the broadsheet press had suggested that our efforts were all the work of one or two sick individuals. Fortunately, this opinion, which would diminish the impact of our efforts were it to become received wisdom, did not appear to be widely held. There were, furthermore, several encouraging mentions of the Devil and Demons from Hell. It was beginning to emerge that one thing which was working enormously in our favour was the nature of the news media themselves. The themes of Evil-at-large, Death-stalking-our-streets made for better stories (Judith Heriot, Press and Publicity Officer, who had been monitoring these developments closely, told us that the correct technical term for this was 'sexier') than did stories about one or two sick or disturbed individuals. All in all, it was concluded, our manipulation of the media had got off to a better start than could have been expected.

3. Strategy for dealing with over-attentive members of press

A number of options for dealing with any journalist (the name of Stuart Brown having been mentioned in this context) who got too close to us with the attendant risk of premature exposure, were discussed, but in the end the favoured option was the abduction of the said individual, our tracks being covered by mind control as in the Post Office mailings, followed by slow roasting on a spit.

4. Further strategy

A number of further strategies were outlined in accordance with our policy of introducing one new strategy per month to run alongside those strategies already in operation. Of those which were discussed, the one which was adopted as being most easily and immediately implemented was the training of our existing agents in the field and, if necessary, the recruitment and training of others, with the purpose of carrying out a programme of desecration. The importance of this programme was two-fold. First, it was symbolic in so far as the Christian church was a symbol, however ineffectual, of some of that which we wished to destroy (though there were also major areas of policy and ideology on which there was complete agreement between ourselves and the Church). Secondly, it would be disruptive, along the same lines as those policies already implemented − a chipping away at the social fabric.

The desecration would take a variety of forms − the daubing of graffiti, the leaving of excrement on altars etc and, in many ways the most important element of the programme, farting in church. All agents would be encouraged to attend church whenever possible (with no regard to denomination) and to fart during services. They would be issued with training manuals detailing the most effective means of producing flatus − the consumption of cabbage, beans, stout beers, German wines etc − and would be allowed to exercise complete discretion in deciding which services to interrupt, the only caveat being it should be done in as loud and unpleasant (in the olfactory sense) a manner as possible.

This element of the policy was also, it was decided, extendible in two ways. First, PISP would take steps to ensure that farting in church became a fashion amongst those elements of the youth of the country which were attracted by the idea of rebellion and subversion. Secondly, it could be extended to the secular realm: a similar effect could be produced by the production of flatus in the presence of Her Majesty the Queen or, in the larger towns and cities of Scotland, the lord provost. Except in Edinburgh, of course, where there would be no need. The Lord Provost of Edinburgh was one of ours. Judith would be able to recruit willing volunteers for this aspect of our operations via her outreach work.

After the main business of the meeting, we had a more leisurely trawl through our press cuttings. This one caught my eye.

'Evil stalks our streets' says exorcist priest

by Stuart Brown

Damien-style priest Father Tom O'Connell, one of Scotland's top exorcists, today slammed the wave of Evil stalking our streets. 'I am sick of this', said Father O'Connell, as he launched an attack on the church and the police for failing to do anything about what he called 'the string of outrages against human decency' which had broken out in recent months.

Calling for the church to make a stand against the 'tidal wave of degeneracy and filth which had beset us', he said that the perpetrator of the recent outrage involving the mutilated remains of upwards of one hundred puppies should be found, and an example should be made of him.

'This is an evil man,' said Father O'Connell, 'and though it may not be fashionable to say so in this day and age, I see the hand of the Devil at work in this.'

Part of the problem, said Father O'Connell, was the amount of sex and violence being shown on the television. Edinburgh was now a cess-pit of degraded humanity, he said. There was pornography everywhere you looked, and so-called 'saunas' and 'massage parlours' on every street corner, but the real cause of the evil stalking our streets was that people had ceased to believe that there was such a thing.

People have forgotten about the devil', he said. 'People have forgotten about God. They take it all very lightly, and unless they mend their ways, they might be very sorry very soon. They must find their faith before it's too late'.

I like this turbulent priest. Very perceptive. But doomed to be ignored, I fear. No-one gives a damn about all that God stuff. Scarcely anyone cares about all that goodness and evil rubbish. Which I why I shall eventually triumph.

PRESS CUTTING

There was another cutting produced at that meeting which caught my eye. It was another interview with this psychologist, the Livesey woman. Meek's met her, by the way, in a professional capacity. She comes to the Royal Edinburgh from time to time to practise, or something. Meek says she's a fool.

This time she obviously felt she had more to go on, because the piece was much longer than the previous one, and she went on at some length about the kind of person who would do the sort of thing which I was doing.

It was one of the quality dailies which spoke to her and asked her to profile me in its features pages. I suppose that, in part, accounts for the length of the piece.

It was still a load of old tosh though.

This is the gist of what the eminent Dr Livesey said, speaking to Grania Robinson-Smith. I shan't bore you with the whole thing.

'The person who did these things is obviously very deeply motivated . . . he must have had a very disturbed childhood. I think that that, in itself, can't explain what he has been doing though. I think that, in these cases, there is more likely to be some proximate or immediate cause, usually a trauma of some kind . . .

'I think that it is obvious that there are some very deep-seated psychological problems at work . . . the fact that animals are being abused in this way tends to support the idea that some sort of power complex is in evidence. This sort of behaviour is associated with some forms of schizophrenia . . .

'I also think that, in purely motivational terms, we can begin to discern a deep-seated hatred of women. Remember that cats in general, kittens in particular, are usually thought of as feminine, or at least as having feminine qualities . . . we use the word 'pussy' to describe the very core of femininity, the most intimate part of a woman . . . and it is worth bearing in mind that last time it was puppies. The similarity between puppy and pussy is very striking in this context, isn't it? . . .'

The empty ravings of a charlatan, of course. I have two observations to make in response to her drivellings.

First, isn't it remarkable that, when someone does something which people regard as evil, or beyond the pale in some way, there is this tendency to look for psychological motivations? Why do people do that? I am not mad. I am Evil.

Second, it is not true that I have a deep-seated hatred of women. Ask Meek or Judith. On second thought, it is true that I have a deep-seated hatred of women, but I have a deep-seated hatred of everybody else, too. I may be Evil, but I'm not a sexist.

He uses these things, the things I told him. He teases me. No. That's the wrong word. Torments me. That's his word. That's what he does. He torments me. He torments me by bringing up the things I told him on that night when he tricked me. Private things. Sometimes he introduces them out of the blue. No warning. Just starts talking about them so he can torment me. In front of other people too. He tells them my deepest secrets. Bastard.

He's told you some of them already. Tormented me by telling you and tormented me by making me write them down.

This is hard for me to write. These things about my shop. About the sweeties. About keeping sweeties in the shop to attract little boys. It's true. I wish it wasn't. I told him about it that Thursday night. I told him in confidence. Now everybody knows. Bastard. I even told him about the photographs. Of me. Of me and. Me and some other people. I almost burned them. They're in a drawer.

I wish I'd kept my mouth shut.

The thing that really makes me angry though is, see if I told anyone things about him, even if it was something really horrible that I had just made up, about him having sex with animals or something, He'd just say 'yes, that's right, it's all true' even if it wasn't, and he'd smile that horrible smile he's got. He's already told you most of the stuff he told me, except the stuff about his wife. He doesn't care what people think about him. He's got no shame. He's evil. He's an evil bastard.

TEST TRANSMISSION

I telephoned Meek the morning after the PISP group meeting and had her meet me for lunch. I had told the group of my plan to start practising in a small way and to build up to the full broadcast gradually, so she had been expecting that I would call on her services to help me practise. She had been very taken with the idea of broadcasting messages with the aim of bringing about Universal Despair from the very first time she heard it, so she was the obvious choice for someone to help me out. I got the distinct impression that she was quite impressed that I called on her services quite so soon after having first mentioned the idea. I'd had to take the credit for having had the idea in the first place, by the way, because I still didn't want the others to know about Torquil.

We met as arranged, a pub on the High Street. My usual haunt. The World's End. I had been drinking there for years, but it had become a curiously apposite place to drink in since I had found out Who I really Was.

I started practising right away. First, just to keep my hand in, before Meek went to the bar to make our food order, I put into her head the knowledge that I wanted the home-made steak and kidney pie. As an afterthought, I also put into her head the notion that she should have the freshly fried scampi in a crispy crumb. This was quite unusual for her as she doesn't really like fish, and there was a moment when I almost regretted this action as it would spoil her lunch, but then I realised that I could easily make her like fish so there was no real problem.

This gave me a bit of confidence.

She had forgotten to ask me what I wanted to drink, so I transmitted my drinks order to her while she was at the bar. No problem. She turned around and smiled, nodding.

After lunch it was time to take the first new step. I went to the toilet and transmitted to Meek from there. This was the first time I had tried to put thoughts into someone else's head without being able to see them. It worked like a charm. By the time I got back to our seats, there was another drink waiting for me.

Since I was doing so well, I decided to take the next step straight away. I targeted the people at the table next to us and willed them to leave. It took me about twenty minutes. I concentrated very hard on them, thinking 'leave, leave, leave, leave, leave' over and over again, and eventually they did. I was tired after expending all this effort, though, so I had to have a breather and a whisky.

Unfortunately, this is where my practice plans went slightly awry. I had been planning, next, to broadcast a message to everyone in the pub, but, by the time I was ready, everyone had left, and the barman, a surly man who, I noted, might make an excellent recruit to our cause, looked as if he was preparing to close the bar. I thought momentarily about willing him to keep the bar open, but decided not to as I had already proved beyond any reasonable doubt that I was quite capable of transmitting thoughts to one person on an individual basis. Larger-scale broadcasting would have to wait.

Though not, as it turned out, for very long.

I'm more of a nurse than a servant, sometimes. He lies there on his bed, drooling and crying, and he expects me to come and hold his hand and make sympathetic noises. I bring him cups of tea, I bring him food, I make sure he puts clean clothes on, I do a thousand and one domestic chores, but most of all what I do is watch him to make sure he's alright.

You'd ask me why I do this when he torments me. Why do I not leave. Go back to Mrs Findlay's. I know she's kept the room for me. Says it's always there if I need it.

I ask this myself, all the time. I don't know. Except I do feel sorry for him, even though he's cruel. Besides, someone's got to take care of him, haven't they. If I didn't make sure that he at least looked as if he was living normally, he'd end up getting locked away or something. They'd take him into care. And they'd charge him for the privilege, seeing as he's got money.

Once in a while, when he's feeling really low, when he's been crying, he'll say 'thankyou' to me. He says it very quietly. In a whisper. But he says it.

TEA-TIME BROADCAST

I arranged for Meek to come over to my house the day after that lunch. I knew the Grocer wouldn't be there – I would send him away on some foolish errand – so we would have the place to ourselves. I'd thought about calling Judith, but it was a question of empathy. I wanted to practise with someone I knew would be receptive.

At the appointed hour she came around, and I went through a series of limbering-up exercises. First, I sat next to her and put thoughts into her head. She put her hand on my crotch, just as I had intended her to do. Then I transmitted to her across the room, but with my face to the wall so that I couldn't see her. 'Yes it is, isn't it?' she replied, so I knew that she'd received the message. Then I moved to the small room next door and transmitted from there. Meek banged on the wall when she got the message (the message being simply 'bang on the wall', a neat solution to the 'how do I know if she's received the message?' dilemma).

I was tired after that, so we had a lie down on the bed, then Meek got up and made us a cup of tea, my seed dribbling down the insides of her thighs. She makes reasonable tea, but I have to say that the Grocer does it better. There you go, I've said something nice about you again. That's twice, I think. I seem to remember having said something quite pleasant about you a few weeks ago. It won't happen again. What I mean to say is that the Grocer makes a good cup of tea considering his moronic inability to do anything else.

Meek, as I say, went off to make a cup of tea. What happened next was extraordinary.

Sometimes you can suddenly discover an ability, or something you have been working at comes right, but does it all of a sudden, not by a gradual improvement. I remember this happening when I was playing tennis as a child. Tired of being beaten again and again, I practised my service for hours and hours and hours, and did so repeatedly. It seemed to make no difference but then, all of a sudden, during a game, I found that I was serving aces.

On this day, the same sort of thing happened. Whilst Meek had been boiling the kettle, warming the pot etc (according to my strict instructions), I had been letting my thoughts wander, not something I usually do, so I fell into a kind of reverie, and accepted the cup of tea she had made me in a dream-like, or perhaps trance-like state. I sipped it absently and suddenly found myself broadcasting my thoughts. What I was thinking at the time was irrelevant. What was important was the fact that I was absolutely positive that the mind of everyone in the Lothians, in Fife, in East Stirlingshire, Clackmannanshire and as far away as Glasgow had been touched by mine. They had all had a message.

As it happened, the content of the message was 'this tea is too strong and there's not quite enough milk in it'. As I say, though, the content of the message was irrelevant. The fact of its having been transmitted was what mattered. It was a very encouraging development. It shows the importance of perseverance.

All I had to do now was learn to control my ability properly. It was going to take a lot of practice, I thought. That was the reason I said to Meek that I thought it might be a good idea if, for the time being at least, she got her stuff and moved in here with me.

THE TRUTH

He's started breeding flies. It's horrible. I hate flies.

There's this room in the house. Just off his bedroom. He calls it the dressing room. It's got no windows. He put this electric fire in there, a three bar one, top of the range, switches on the side for controlling the temperature. He keeps it very warm in there, and he leaves meat and sugar on the table. I stood by the door once. It stinks. Every other day, he goes in there with a fishing net, like a kiddie would use (probably stole it off some kiddie) and some jam jars, and comes out with all these flies.

I won't go in there. I hate flies. Always have. You have to when you're a greengrocer. They crawl all over your produce, make it filthy. People won't buy it. Flies are the greengrocer's worst enemy. Apart from the VAT man, and the public.

What he does with the jam jars is this. He takes them, in his briefcase – he always looks respectable when he wants to, and when I've brushed his suit and ironed him a shirt – and goes into banks, building societies, libraries, department stores and so on, gets a jar out of the briefcase, unscrews the lid and leaves it hidden somewhere. He's spending a lot of time at the moment in Jenner's. He likes leaving his jars of flies in the haberdashery department on Tuesdays, cookware on Thursdays, and the foodhall on Saturday when it's busiest.

He says he aims to increase the fly population in major public spaces a hundredfold within four years. I asked why and he said 'Because I can.'

There were more stories in the papers when the deep-fried kittens had all been delivered. They realised it was a repeat of the puppies thing. STOP THIS SICKO just about sums up the tone of the tabloid coverage. An interesting feature of the coverage was that, though the story with the 'stop the sicko' headline did, as before, mention the Bag of Limbs incident (para 12), the focus of the moral outrage was most definitely on the suffering of the poor little baby animals.

Inspector Gordon Allan of the Lothian and Borders Police got his ugly, pinched face on the news again. He was all over the tea-time television news. Some viewers may find this report shocking..

He gave a news conference. He got grilled, but by no means was he toasted. The press were very hostile, and he kept saying things like 'I would like to assure you and the public that we are doing our utmost to apprehend this sick individual, preferably before any further outrage is committed'.

They asked him questions. On the television news bulletin which I saw, the questions themselves were inaudible, but his replies were:

1) 'Yes, I am aware of the allegations that there has been some Satanic element to these horrific acts. This is, obviously, one of the lines along which our investigations are proceeding.'

2) 'I am not prepared to say, but I will read a brief statement concerning the suspect who has, at this moment in time, been detained by us in relation to our enquiries: [looks down at paper and reads in stilted fashion] We have

detained a post office employee, Mrs Anne Alloway, of Ormiston Terrace, Edinburgh, who has been arrested and is facing a number of charges. We have had no choice but to believe her guilty of, at the very least, complicity in this outrage as she has been able to supply us with no satisfactory or credible explanation for her allowing the 76 kittens to have been posted from her counter at the post office, and has, to the contrary, been most obstructive in her dealings with us. It is our belief that she may be trying to protect some person or persons unknown, and any person having information with regard to any suspicious or suspect persons with whom Mrs Alloway is known to associate should contact either myself or one of my officers immediately.'

3) 'I am not prepared to comment on allegations in the press and certain other quarters that either the post office itself, or a conspiracy of those working within it, is somehow involved.'

4) 'Yes, there was a message enclosed with all the parcels which have so far been reported to us. The message reads [fumbles for second piece of paper and reads in similar fashion] 'Tremble ye and weep. Fall upon your knees. Cover your eyes. For He is coming.' The h of he is a capital. It is typewritten on high-quality notepaper. We are, at the present moment in time, unsure as to the meaning of the message. Any persons having any information as to the meaning of the message or the identity of the perpetrator are invited to contact myself or Sergeant Tom McCall at Lothian and Borders Police Headquarters.'

CONVENIENCE – ANOTHER ADVANTAGE OF EVIL

Before I was Revealed to Myself, I was a slave to my stomacho-colonic reflex. Every time I ate something I would, fifteen minutes later, find myself sitting upon the toilet, passing stool. Now I am Revealed as the Antichrist, however, I find I am much less concerned with the evacuation of waste matter from my bowel. Sometimes a week or more may pass without my paying a visit. As I become a more spiritual, less corporeal, being, I expect this trend will continue and grow. Eventually I shall be able to dispense with that tiresome aspect of my being altogether.

NEWS IRONY

I can't have been the only person to have noticed the irony of the report of my feline activities in Stuart Brown's paper being placed opposite a report complaining about the huge increase over the past ten years in the number of feral cats in Edinburgh and Glasgow. Other papers ran the two stories on the same day, too. What the Dark Lord taketh away, He also giveth back.

Ha.

He disappears some times on what he calls his errands of mercilessness. Usually he's just going to the office. I look forward to these times. I get away from him for a wee while. He's been very gloomy recently. He was never cheerful, but he's really taken a turn for the worse these last few weeks.

I've never seen him smile.

It's quite nice when Gillian's here. I can talk to her. I don't mind her at all.

And when I'm at the shop, I get away from him then too, though he lets me get out to open up less and less often. People are complaining. They come into the shop and say, 'You're hardly ever open these days Mr Borthwick.' I tell them there's something wrong at home. Looking after a sick relative, so they understand. Most of them. But it's hard to keep a good turnover of stock going when you're hardly ever open and you don't know when you'll get back to open up and people aren't coming anyway because the shop on the next corner is more reliable. It's bad for business.

Guidelines on the Implementation of Evil

The enemies of Evil

1. The enemies of Evil are legion. Do-gooders, philanthropists, socialists, liberals, charity workers. Remember however, that

the institutions – Church and State, the forces of law and order, etc – are not included here. They can be made to work for us. Indeed, this is our goal.

2. The Antichrist Himself is always in mortal danger from many sources. Lunatics, religious maniacs, moral guardians.

3. He must be protected at all costs if the Implementation of Evil is to succeed. His Person is the one person that is of any importance.

THE GROCER ASKS A QUESTION

The Grocer wants to ask me a question. He's just asked me if he can ask me something. Well I never. Actually, you can put an exclamation mark after that never. I don't usually approve of them, they're so vulgar, but you can use one just this once, seeing it's a special occasion. Go for it.

Well I never!

Yes, you can ask me a question, though I am, I confess, quite surprised that you have found the courage to do so. What has got into you?

The question he has just asked me is 'If you're the Antichrist, why are you wasting so much time having sexual relations with Gillian and Judith?'

Sexual relations?

Gillian? Gillian, is it? Does she know you're calling her Gillian? I've seen the way you look at her, but I wasn't aware that you had gone the whole hog and actually spoken to her. What a brave little man. All of a sudden. You've started asking questions, and you've plucked up the courage to speak to Meek. I bet she gave you the old brush off though. Ignored you. Maybe told you to go and boil your turnip head.

Thought so.

Still.

To answer your question, then. Where does it say that I shouldn't have girlfriends, just because I'm the Antichrist? Especially if the girls I'm having sexual relations with are my trusted lieutenants. Do you seriously think that the boy Jesus didn't have sexual relations with that prostitute he was hanging about with. What's the point of hanging around with a prostitute if you don't? What's the point of hanging around with any woman?

Sorry, that sounded sexist, and, by implication, homophobic. What's the point of hanging around with anyone attractive, unless you have sexual relations with them?

That's better.

I bet the boy Jesus had carnal knowledge of all his associates. Messiahs are good at everything. If he was anything like me I bet he could make the Earth move. I bet he exhausted them all. I bet there's some double meaning in that story about how Peter denied him three times before cock-crow.

Besides, who says having sexual relations is a waste of time?

In a way, you know, I am glad that you have found the nerve to question me. It shows at least a degree of spirit where I thought you had none. Well done. However, I am going to have to punish you for your impertinence. Take down your trousers.

Yes, write that down too.

And this. This is going to hurt.

You can stop now.

BATTERED BABY

I was reading the morning paper, scanning it for more reports of our activities, to whit the deep-fried kittens. There was a report on our feline outrage, and there were a number of stories which caught my eye. It had been seeming that, lately, almost everything which was not about the private life of some famous or not-so-famous-but-perhaps-you-might-have-heard-of-them person was about evil or moral degeneracy. It was all, as I say, most encouraging. The fact that people were thinking that the moral, social and physical fabric of society was decaying, even if this was not true, was making our task much easier.

Then I came across a story which caught my eye even more than the others. '**Scotland is battered baby capital of Europe**' it read. This gave me an idea for my next project.

I told Meek of a plan that was developing in my head. She heard it as it was being formulated, and she was very impressed. 'Gosh, Hector,' she said. 'You are a very nasty man.' She was chuckling. I was not as amused myself. I doubted there was anything I could do to cheer myself up. Meek agreed to procure what we needed from the hospital mortuary that afternoon. I, for my part, would procure eggs, flour, milk and salt. It meant going down Easter Road to the shops, which is never pleasant, but we all have our crosses to bear.

We set out at the back of midnight, in the car, on the

road to West Lothian. I wasn't feeling terribly enthusiastic, and the A71 is not a road designed to buck up your spirits. I was wondering whether we would actually achieve anything significant that night. The Grocer had sparked off a chain of thought that was driving me deeper and deeper into a chasm of gloom. And I hadn't been very happy to start off with. Was I just wasting my time? Was I ever going to achieve anything?

It was only one o'clock when we pulled up outside the Marinara fish 'n' chicken bar, so we had to hang around for a while as there were still one or two people about. At a quarter past two, we entered the Marinara by the same means as I had previously, and switched on one of the fryers.

As the fat was heating, Meek and I prepared a large bowl of batter mix, and coated the body of the baby she had brought in her bag in flour and egg white, to make sure that the batter would stick. We also peeled and chipped some three pounds of potatoes.

When the fat was hot enough, we popped the newly battered baby into the fryer, along with the chips. It took a mere ten minutes, and, having seasoned the baby with salt, vinegar and sauce, and wrapped it with the chips in newspaper, we were back out on the street at three. It smelled delicious, and made us both very hungry. However, you have to ignore the demands of the body when you are on a mission for Evil.

Guidelines on the Implementation of Evil

Sexual activity

1. Sexual activity, and the urges which accompany it, is one of our strongest weapons.

2. The good are driven to indulge in sexual activity, but the vast majority of them look upon the urge to do so as a manifestation of Evil, and therefore as something to be resisted.

3. Most of them are, however, powerless to resist. Evidence of this can be found in the success of the advertising industry, which harnesses the sexual impulses for its own ends.

4. The conflict between their impulses and their attitudes towards their impulses is one of their chief weaknesses.

5. We must exploit this weakness.

6. We must be more like an advertising agency.

THE TRUTH

He locked me in the room with the flies. He made me take my clothes off and smear jam on myself, then he made me go into the room and locked me in. I was there for hours. It was horrible. They were crawling all over me. There were millions of them. When there's that many there's nothing you can do to keep them off. You can brush one or two off, but there are always too many. In the end I just had to sit in the corner and let them land on me. There was no furniture in there. No toilet. That was the first time I have cried since I was at school.

KID SUPPER

We took the battered baby back to Edinburgh, laughing in the car about the idea of going into a chip shop and asking for Kid and chips. We discussed the possibility of other applications of the same principal. Babyburger and fries. Infant Tikka Masala. Penne alla bambino. Sweet and sour child with egg-fried rice. Then we did it with christian names. Pan-fried Peter, Martin marinee, Susie sushi, John jam, James jam, Paul puree, Jugged Jane, Sara sautee in a Colin coulis, Louise a l'orange, Dickon Kiev, Rebecca roulade, Pete Wellington, Pete Melba, Keith Bourgignon, Graham Masala, Dick a l'orange, Bombay Dick, crispy aromatic Peking Dick with traditional Chinese pancakes, stir-fried Stephanie, Sasha sate, Donna kebab. This kept us amused for the whole journey home.

We got back to Edinburgh at twenty-to-four, and it hardly seemed worth going to bed as there was more work to do first thing in the morning. We decided that we'd get some kip during the day, after breakfast, so we stayed up the rest of the night making more jokes about children, and reliving the way the fat had spat when we put the baby in, how it had changed colour, how it had smelled when it was done. We were feeling rather pleased with ourselves. It was the one time I remember feeling anything like happy. Meek is very good at making me forget myself.

At eight that morning we put the supper into a small cardboard box – a shoe box, as it happens – along with a note saying 'behold ye and tremble and fall down upon your knees, for He is coming and He is The Beast' underneath which was a little thing that Meek had thought up which read simply 'suffer the little children'. Underneath this was yet another note, this one cut out from a Bird's Eye Menu Masters packet, which said 'to enjoy piping hot, remove contents from wrapping and heat in microwave on full power for 3 mins'.

I took the package to the office of a courier firm on London Road, not far from my house, and told them to ferry it to the headquarters of Dr Barnado's, the children's charity. I got some bacon and some rolls on the way back. When I got back I rang Judith and asked her to meet us at the house. She arrived when we had just changed into our jim-jams and were sitting down to breakfast. The Grocer let her in and she came through to the kitchen. She looked at us and said, 'Very cosy.' I was too tired to ask what she meant. I simply told her what we'd done and asked her to arrange the press coverage, give the journalists Barnardos' phone number and promise them the before-and-after snapshots we'd taken.

I DIDN'T SLEEP VERY WELL

Meek and I went to bed. She fell into a sound sleep. Being a nurse, she can sleep anywhere and in any state. Nurses have to be able to do this, otherwise they don't get any sleep.

Me, I need conditions to be right. That day they weren't.

For one thing, it was daylight, and there were chinks in the curtains. For another, we'd just had a hearty breakfast of bacon rolls, and I can never sleep on a full stomach.

I did doze of eventually. No sooner had I done so than I started dreaming. I dreamt of the journalist Kirsty Wark, long an idol of mine. This was no erotic dream, though. Ms Wark was chairing a discussion on fiscal policy in which the studio audience was giving vent to its anger about the burden of high taxation. Suddenly I heard a familiar voice miaowing 'Taxing? You call that taxing. I can tell you about taxing. Just ask me. You should have my worries. Where I live it's a rise one day, a rise the next . . .'

Knowing what was going to happen, I woke up. Torquil was sitting by the bedside. He said, 'Arise, arise. Get out of your bed already. There's things to do.' Meek was still fast asleep.

I scowled at him. 'Ahh. Who's my little ray of sunshine, then?' he said.

I asked him what he wanted.

'Nothing,' he said.

'You woke me up,' I said. 'I haven't slept for 36 hours. I'm very tired and I don't feel very well.'

'Alright, alright,' he said. 'So I'll make it snappy. Try to do the boy a favour, this is how he repays me. Come with a warning, he bites my head off. This sort of trouble I could do without.'

'Warning?' I asked.

'Oh, so now he's interested. I tell him there's a warning and suddenly he's all ears. Wouldn't give me the time of day before.'

'Please tell me about this warning,' I said.

'Very polite. I like that. Very polite. That's good.'

'Please?'

'OK. You're sure you're listening?'

'Yes.'

'OK. Your father, he's not happy. The trouble you give him. As if he hasn't got worries enough. Thousands of years he's worked to give you a decent world to rule over, and what do you care? How do you repay him? By messing about with your friends when you should be out running the world. Well he's angry, I should tell you. You should see his face. The disappointment, oy, it's breaking his heart. Yesterday he speaks to me, he says, Torquil, go to the boy, go to him tell him from me that I'm going to teach him a lesson. Tell him in a few days, a few weeks, I'm going to have the stuffing knocked out of him, take him right out of there and teach him a lesson he'll never forget. That's all. You've got a few days, a few weeks. Get your act together. The mood he's in he's going to do something terrible to you.'

He pointed his paw at me and wagged it up and down, shaking his head in disapprobation. He was making a tutting noise. He gradually faded from view. I rolled onto my side and put my arm around Meek. I couldn't believe that she had slept through all that. She *was* very tired.

I was very depressed.

A WALK IN THE PARK

Meek is the closest to me of all my servants. She is the one thing in my life that keeps me sane. She has come closest to understanding True Evil, even though she was not born to

Evil. Unlike myself, or Judith. Whereas I am blessed with a wisdom which surpasses all others, and Judith is the proud owner of a cold streak and a ruthless cunning, Meek has a knowledge of men and women which is deep. She is already perceptive, but one day I shall teach her to look deep into their souls and see their secrets. Whereas I can reach out to the stars and feel the Universe, draw the Life, the Fire from it, and leave it withered and shrivelled like a month-old peach, destroy any of its creatures with a flick of my finger, she too has great power.

She knows now that Evil is Real. When first I met her she did not truly believe. She went along with me because she trusted me and because I could do things for her, but now she can feel Evil. She can feel it deep inside her. It spurts through her veins. She can touch it and taste it in her mouth, just as I can. It has a sweet, sweet, taste, and it makes her shiver and tremble with Joy.

This is a mark of how much I care for her. The day after Torquil's visit, she and I went for a walk in Princes Street Gardens. I told her about what had happened. 'Gillian,' I said, 'you know little of this, but there shall soon come a day when, our work being almost wholly implemented, I shall be no longer among you. I shall have to be taken from you that I may arise again, more powerful than before.'

She was upset by this, for she is quite devoted to me. She said, 'Don't be a silly old Hector. No-one's going to take you away from me. Don't say such things. You are powerful and you could easily destroy any enemies who threaten you. You could stay with me forever and we could rule the earth together.'

I told her what Torquil had said, and explained how I saw it. 'My Task upon the Earth,' I said, 'is to bring about an Everlasting Reign of Terror. In order for this outcome to be implemented, I must be taken from you. I do not yet know how this will happen, only that it must be so, for this my Father has told me. It is only thus that I can destroy Goodness forever. Can you not see that, though we have achieved much that is Evil, it is as nothing?'

She started crying. I took her head in my hands and said to her, 'I have a reason for telling you this now.'

She looked up at me expectantly and I said to her 'Gillian, if and when I am gone, another must take over the Network of Evildoers. If it happens, I shall be remote, I shall need a lieutenant. That shall be you, for of all my servants and companions and my army of followers, you are the closest to my heart. You are my Peter, my Right Hand, my Spock, my Boswell, my amanuensis, my Watson. When I am gone, you, Meek, shall inherit the Earth.'

Then, because I had much to contemplate, I said to her, 'Go now. Leave me here in this garden. Go and think on what I have told you. Then tell that silly little half rotted beetroot faced arse of a bastard grocer to get my Book ready.'

Guidelines on the Implementation of Evil

On the Bodily nature of Evil

1. Most practitioners of Evil notice that much of the Evil which is being practised in this current regime concerns people and their bodies.

2. There is nothing new about this. Evil has always been a largely corporeal phenomenon.

3. This is not because of a lack of imagination on the part of the practitioners.

4. It is because human beings are obsessed, physical, animal creatures. In this sense, there is no difference between them and the dogs and cats they keep as pets.

5. The crucial difference, of course, is that human beings can understand pain and suffering, whilst dogs and cats merely experience it. This makes human beings much easier to terrorise.

THE TRUTH

I'm angry.

Sometimes I think I hate her just as much as I hate him. I used to think she was nice, but now I think I hate her. She dotes on him. It makes me sick. She lets him put his thing in her. She's like a puppy in his lap.

Why does he give her so much attention? She's pretty, but she does fuck all. Does she write his precious stupid book for him? No. Does she cook his meals? Does she fetch and carry for him? Does she make sure he looks presentable when he goes out?

No.

She understands him.

Ha.

Odd jobs, that's all she does.

What about that wank about her being his Peter, his right hand. What about Judith? What about me? She's not his right hand. Though that would explain the stains on her clothes. I do all the work. I do all the shitty jobs. But I get none of the credit. Not even a thankyou.

Bastards. Bastards, the pair of them.

SMALL EARTHQUAKE

Within its limited horizons, my latest initiative was a success. The battered baby got us several headlines. Judith did very well, though it did very little to lift my mood. Still, I might as well quote one of the stories the baby thing gave rise to. For what it's worth I'll quote the one by our old friend Mr Brown, as it was much the same as any of the others. I quote him since he did so well out of us. Our story helped his career along in no small way. It's from of The *Scotsman* dated 5th August. It doesn't really mean very much.

'Battered Baby' horror cops have few leads

by *Stuart Brown, chief reporter*

Police and forensic scientists working on the so-called 'Battered Baby' case have established that the baby dipped in batter, deep-fried and delivered to the headquarters of top children's charity Dr Barnardo's on Monday was that of little Martin Lee.

Tragic Martin died shortly after being born at Edinburgh's Eastern General Hospital on Saturday night. Despite numerous phone calls to their house yesterday, his rieving parents were said by a family friend to be too upset to make any comment. It is believed that Martin's body was chosen by the perpetrator of the outrage for reasons of convenience rather than as a deliberate act of hostility towards the Lees.

An investigation is currently underway into how Martin's body came to be stolen, but sources within the police have admitted that they are, at the moment, 'clueless'. Hospital staff have, so far, been unable to identify the place where the body was stolen from, as it has not been established whether it had yet been taken to the mortuary for storage prior to the routine post-mortem examination which was due to have been carried out on Sunday morning.

The only additional leads in the case have come from top psychologist Dr Mary Livesey, who has been helping the police to compile a profile of the perpetrator of this outrage and the previous incidents involving small mammals.

Speaking yesterday, Dr Livesey said that the individual the police were looking for obviously had a deep-seated hatred of children, women and animals, the roots of which possibly lie in his own childhood. 'This is a complex and very dangerous man,' she said. 'The degree of organisation he has shown, and the imagination, are a particularly effective combination. One almost admires his efficiency and daring'.

All this publicity, and this was just one of many, many stories written that day, was all very well, but I couldn't help thinking that I was just messing about. Just as Torquil had said. Was what we had done really Evil? It wasn't very pleasant, I knew that, but was it Evil?

Strangely, although I was the very Embodiment of Evil, I found that I had no way of knowing where Evil started and wickedness stopped, where malice began, what was mere mischief. In a sense, of course, because I was Evil, everything I did was, technically, Evil, but from an objective point of view . . . where was that crucial boundary? And I was thinking about what the Grocer had asked me about Edinburgh. I still had no answer to his question. It had shaken me. That bastard, insignificant, turnip-headed lump of excreta had shaken me.

I had to get a grip, take stock of my strengths. I knew

in my heart of hearts, my cold grey heart, that Evil is essentially a function of government, of huge, powerful organisations, of bureaucracies. That's the whole point of the guidelines. It's about administration. We were, it's true, big in the City of Edinburgh District Council (Improving Services, Creating Torment) and were exerting a large degree of influence in the Scottish Office, but somehow this just wasn't . . . big enough. It was getting us nowhere. And yet I had so much potential. I was frittering it away. I was frustrated, hemmed in, aware of my inadequacy.

It was a line of thought that kept me occupied for many hours. The hours turned into days, then into weeks. I sank into a black mood. I experienced a feeling of complete failure. My whole life had been a waste of time.

I was aware that I was waiting for something to happen, something which would transform me. But I didn't know what. Inspiration, perhaps. I had to expand my limited vision. I didn't know how, and I didn't know what I was supposed to become.

In the end I decided that the only thing I could do, indeed, what I had been doing all along, was explore the boundaries of Evil by pushing them out as far as possible. Keep working towards it, inching towards it. It would do in the meantime. For want of something better.

Until the something that was going to happen happened. Whatever it was.

Something happened, all right, but not really the way I'd planned it.

I was called in to see the heid bummer at the Scottish Office two days later. Chief Executive. Head of the whole show. One up from me in the chain of command. Very grand office, very big desk. We talked about the weather, my health. He even started to ask about my wife, but stopped himself just in time. Then he said to me, 'Hector, you've done a lot of very valuable work over the years, and you've risen remarkably quickly. You're the youngest Head of Department we've ever had. you're still only, what 37? Yes, you just turned 37 what, eight weeks ago? Maybe you've risen a little too quickly, burnt yourself out.'

He stared off into space for a few minutes with his fingertips pressed together under his nose. Then he said 'I'm afraid we're going to have to let you go. You've been under too much strain recently and it's been showing in your work. I've got a full dossier here, and I'm afraid that it doesn't make very pretty reading.' He patted a big buff file on his desk. 'We won't go into details, and there's certainly no need to discuss how I got hold of this dossier, but I think you know the sort of thing I'm talking about.'

There was a pause. An atmosphere. He put a concerned look on his face. 'We'll give you three months salary to tide you over, and you'll get excellent references of course. There's no need to go back to your office, take the rest of the day off. I'll have Miss Heriot send your things on. She'll be taking over your duties.'

The presumption. How dare he? Sack me? Me? I was furious.

This was a big setback. Obviously. Access to the Scottish Office bureaucracy was going to have been one of my biggest assets. There's nothing quite like being a big cheese in a bureaucracy when you want to take over the world and do it some serious harm.

NO RESPONSE FROM JUDITH

I was distraught. Of all the things that could have happened, this was the final blow. The Reign of Terror was getting nowhere. I couldn't even hold on to my job at the Scottish Office.

I tried to telephone Judith when I finally got home. The bus ride had seemed to take forever. I was in a daze, there was an enormous weight on my shoulders. I was told she wasn't taking calls because she was in the process of moving office. I tried to leave a message on her answerphone at home, but it wasn't switched on.

The following things flashed though my mind:

Was it just a coincidence that she was taking over my duties at the Scottish Office?

Was it just a coincidence that she was moving offices? (Into mine, I supposed.)

There was no way for me to tell. I had my suspicions though.

THE PIT OF DESPAIR AND PRINCES STREET

I was inconsolable. I was by turns raging and withdrawn. Meek and the Grocer avoided me. Not that I cared. I didn't want to speak to anyone.

I locked myself in my room. I didn't eat for a week. I just lay there thinking about what had happened to me. My whole life didn't so much flash before my eyes as saunter and dawdle, mooning at me, mocking me with its pathetic tragedies. I thought about my parents, about how my wife had died, how I'd been saddled with the burden of being Evil Incarnate, how I'd lost my job, how I didn't know whether I could trust my friends. I thought about how I really ought to be able to cope with this sort of thing if I were the Embodiment of Evil. I thought about how little I'd achieved, despite all the advantages of my birth. I thought about the Reign of Terror and how it was no closer now than it had been when I'd started. It all seemed too much. I cried for days. I was in the Pit of Despair. I decided to end it all.

I had been in my room for eight days. I listened for signs of movement in the house. There weren't any. Meek was at work, I realised, and the Grocer was away on some pathetic little errand. I went into the bathroom and ran the bath. I switched the light over the mirror on, and looked for a way to get a power supply into the bathroom. I noticed the shavers-only socket on the light. I knew there was a two-pin adapter that would fit it in the hall cupboard. I got the electric fire from my dressing room.

I brought the items through into the bathroom, plugged

the adapter into the light socket and the fire into the adapter. I got undressed and got into the bath. I leant over and picked up the fire, took a deep breath and switched it on.

Everything went black. I had expected this, but I had expected to be dead. The lights had blown. My bathroom, being *en suite*, is internal. It has no windows. I couldn't see a thing. I shouted 'BASTARD!' at the top of my voice and tried to get out of the bath. I put one foot on the floor and tripped over the fire. I fell and cracked my head heavily against the sink.

It was the worst moment of my life. I couldn't even end it. I pulled on some clothes. I was still dripping wet. I was confused. I didn't know what the hell was going on. I ran out of the house. I ran down Regent Terrace, down Regent Road and onto Princes Street. I didn't know where I was going, and I couldn't really see properly anyway. I just wanted to run. I wanted to run to the point of exhaustion, so that I wouldn't have to think about what had been happening to me, so that I wouldn't have to face the fact that I was a pathetic failure. Everything I touched turned to shit.

I had no idea what time of day it was, but it must have been in the afternoon. The street was crowded with tourists, shoppers and festival goers. It was desperately hard to make any headway, but I desperately wanted to run, to fly, to get away from the thoughts in my head. I pushed and shoved against the crowds for one block and ran out onto South St Andrews Street and into the path of an oncoming taxi. Its horn blared but I kept going and it screeched to a halt. I crossed the road and stepped onto the pavement outside Jenners. It was even more crowded than the last stretch. I found myself unable to move at more than a snail's pace, even with pushing, kicking and shouting at the insignificant, puny little vermin infesting my path to get out of the way. The pressing crowd became too much for me. I couldn't move at all. It was the very worst moment of my life. I wanted to destroy all the little people. I threw my arms up in the air and screamed. A long, deep howl of Despair. GET OUT OF MY FUCKING WAY! There was a rumble of thunder and a flash of lightning. I swear the earth shook slightly. The people around me cowered back in fear. A space opened up around me.

All of a sudden I felt curiously calm. And much more powerful. Rage. Rage was making me a monster, something to fear, something Terrible to behold.

I had an idea.

Guidelines on the Implementation of Evil

Rage

1. Anger, rage, ire are essential elements of evil.

2. Whereas administration is a method, and violence a tool, rage is a motive.

3. Without a motive you can't do anything.

I knew now that it was time for action. Serious action. I was a mass of rage, I felt the need for an outlet, I felt tremendously powerful. I had decided on some horrific and brutal violence, the only question was what, exactly? I needed some help to get my mind focused.

I called the PISP group together. Only Meek and the Grocer were there on time, having no distance to travel, but I was so full of energy that I decided to start anyway. I was unsure whether Judith would even come. It was a way of testing her. If she didn't come, I knew she'd betrayed me. If she came, everything was alright, she was still on our side, and at least we had a friend in the Scottish Office.

I informed the assembled officers of the course events had taken recently, and that, having weighed up the various options, I had decided on a course of random and horrifically brutal violence. My intentions were still unformed at that point, but, as I was speaking, a plan began to come together in my head. I outlined it, and asked for their comments. Judith came in as I started doing so.

I was pleased, but I carried on without pausing. What I was planning, I told them, was a programmed series of events which I thought we should call 'Sudden Dismemberment Incidents' (to be shortened to SDIs in accordance with the PISP group's corporate style). The programmed series was to be implemented as soon as an appropriate mechanism and set of procedures was identified. The basic premise was that bringing about a destabilising onset of mass panic in the population at large would be greatly facilitated by the perceived or real threat of sudden, terrible, violent and entirely arbitrary death. Based on this premise, my idea was that certain people – targets would be set to determine numbers – chosen completely at random, though with a fair balance between the genders and various ethnic groups, would be suddenly torn apart as if by invisible wild dogs. This would happen in the street, in full view of other members of the public. Indeed, this was vital to the success of the undertaking – the more members of the public who saw it, the better from our point of view, as this would encourage the spread of panic and the belief that Evil stalked the streets.

My initial aim would be to set a target of, say, five Sudden Dismemberment Incidents per week. This seemed to me to be a number which balanced the conflicting aims of, on the one hand, significance in the public mind and, on the other, manageability. My initial thoughts were that, given a successful SDI programme, the public at large would become deeply receptive to our message, and to the next stage in the Implementation of Evil, in as little as three weeks given a) a means of ensuring that my/our responsibility for the SDIs was acknowledged and b) a mechanism for effecting the SDIs was identified and perfected.

I told the assembled officers that the basic tool for effecting the dismemberments – my will – was already in place (and had been for some considerable time), but that it had recently been augmented by the acquisition of Rage. This Rage, when focused, would bring an extra dimension to my activities and allow me to effect incidents at a much higher level of activity than had previously been the case.

It would require considerable practice, of course, starting perhaps on a selection of vegetables and progressing on to small animals, cats, dogs and sheep before dismembering the first human target, but I now had no doubt whatsoever about my ultimate ability to reach out with my will and rend a person limb from limb. The problem, as I saw it, would be in identifying the target, and ensuring that there were witnesses enough to be sure of making the desired impact.

One solution to this which was suggested was to station Meek and Judith at strategic locations, on the High Street say, with walkie-talkies so they could report back to me, giving me the precise co-ordinates and bearing of the targets they identified. I was quite confident of their abilities to do this, but it was pointed out that there were a certain number of logistical problems associated with this course of action. Chief among these was the possibility of identification by the earthly authorities. They would be sure to be called in, and it would come to their attention eventually that every time one of these SDIs took place there was an attractive girlie with a radio in the vicinity.

Another solution which was suggested was the possibility of installing closed-circuit television cameras in a few strategic locations. This had the advantage of being less likely to draw the attention of the earthly authorities – they would not think there was anything untoward about such a system being installed, indeed, they would probably welcome the innovation. However, PISP was forced to reject this course of action also, on the grounds of its expense and inflexibility. To ensure maximum exposure and impact we had to make sure that there was a wide spread of dismemberments.

In the end it was decided that the most practical means of identifying SDI targets was for me to reach out with my will, in surveillance rather than broadcast mode, and, having identified one, switch over to destruct mode. This seemed an efficient, economical strategy, its only disadvantage being that it would require even more practice on my part. However, it was a sacrifice I was all too willing to make if it would further the Implementation of Evil and take me further down the road to the Reign of Terror. The only major frustration was the further delay this would cause.

Judith had remained silent during this meeting. At the end, when I asked her opinion of what had been discussed, she looked at me, then she looked at Meek. She narrowed her eyes and she breathed out heavily through her nose. Then she said, 'I think it's fucking stupid', and left.

Despite this, I began to feel a bit more relaxed. I was doing something. I was worried about Judith, obviously, but I was doing something.

THE TRUTH

This is important. This is the most important thing I've ever told you.

I've got another reason for looking forward to the times when he leaves me alone. I used to, anyway. I've been going back to see Mrs Findlay. One or two nights a week. Funny thing – now I'd moved out of her house, we were getting on very well.

I had to sneak off to visit her because I knew that He wouldn't like it if he knew. He told me once he thought Mrs Findlay was a wicked old hag, even though he'd never met her. He just said it because I'd said something nice about her. I told him he was acting like a jealous woman, and he flew into a rage. Hit the roof. I never mentioned her in front of him again.

Anyway, I'd been seeing her for months. Practically ever since I moved out. She came into the shop one day. We went for tea at a cafe – same one as I went to with him – and started talking. Talking like we'd never talked before. She asked me round for my tea the next Tuesday, and I said yes.

Anyway, after a few months of meeting like this, in the shop or at her house for supper, we started talking about getting married. She wanted to get married in the same kirk as she'd been married in last time. Somewhere in West Lothian, and have the reception – small, not too many people – at the same hotel. I said I didn't mind. We'd even half-fixed a date.

Then, yesterday, I went to see her and she seemed much cooler. Distant. Wouldn't talk to me.

Then she said, 'I had a visit from a friend of yours this morning. Very interesting things he had to say. Told me I was making a mistake in seeing you. Knew we were getting married, told me to call it off. Asked me if I knew the man I was planning to marry was a pervert. Showed me some photographs. Disgusting. Disgusting little man.'

I pretended I didn't know what she meant. But it was no use. She had the photographs. I don't know how she got them.

Yes I do.

She threw them at me and screamed, 'Get out, get out, I never want to see you again!'

Bastard.

PROVERBS

I sometimes find that, when passing on the Essence of Evil to my children, and trying to ensure that they understand me properly, it helps to formulate some of what I have to say in pithy little phrases. A bit like proverbs. I'm putting a few in here, a few of the best ones, as they may help you understand and remember what it is I'm talking about. You can use them as *aides-memoire*, mnemonics. They are derived from various well-known source documents.

Let him that is with sin cast the first stone, him cast many more, and then let him go in with a baseball bat or pick-axe handle.

There are, as I have shown, many ways to get a camel through the eye of a needle. A selection of power tools helps.

Suffer the little children.

Forgive me, Father, for I have not yet sinned enough. I must try harder.

The quality of mercy is not of much use.

There is a tide in the affairs of man, and we are the undertow.

Your Arse, your Arse, my Big Dong up your Arse.

fool and his body are easily parted.

You can lead a horse to water, but drowning it without getting wet takes a very special skill.

SPLATTER

The SDI practice went surprisingly well. I found I was growing stronger in Evil thanks to my Rage.

My first attempts were made in the kitchen. I lined up some tomatoes. I made myself angry with them. Little red bastards. I reached out for them with my will. Little red bastards that stain your clothes and taste of nothing these days. I went inside them and felt their pips. I squeezed them, then I pulled them apart, I found that I could splatter them with a minimum expenditure of effort.

After that I tried melons. Big round bastards. Bastards. Hate them, hate them. Same result. Didn't even take any more effort than the tomatoes. They made a very satisfactory plopping noise as they burst open, and the flesh flew in every direction at once, making a big mess that I was obliged to make the Grocer clean up.

I thought I would then try turnips. Dirty bastards. Dirty bastards my mother used to make me eat though she knew I hated them. Still hate them. I thought they might by harder to burst because they are harder in texture. Less juicy. Obviously, there wasn't so much splattering, but they ripped apart anyway.

So did the hamster. Little furry bastard. Pointless little furry bastard in its stupid little smelly cage. And the cat.

People were going to be no problem at all. The bastards.

Something occurred to me.

I could combine my gifts. I could put thoughts into someone's head while they are being dismembered.

I imagine a severed head doesn't die straight away. It

must stay alive for a good forty seconds, maybe longer, until the oxygen in the brain is all used up. I could plant thoughts into the head I'd just ripped off someone, Reveal myself to them in all My Evil. Confront them with their own puny insignificance, and give them a final moment of Absolute Terror.

Or make their final thought something infuriating but absolutely pointless. Make them go out with that frustrated feeling of not being able to remember something. 'What's the name for that goat's-milk cheese covered in oatmeal?' That sort of thing. Most amusing.

Maybe I'll try it on you, you worthless piece of dung.

Guidelines on the Implementation of Evil

Violence

1. It is not necessary to be violent to be Evil, but it helps. People understand violence. (See 'the Bodily nature of Evil').

2. It is not per se the death or the mutilation or the pain which in themselves are terrible.

3. What really puts the willies into people is the human ability to conceptualise pain and suffering and death, to deal with it in the abstract.

4. This makes it much harder to deal with in reality.

5. For the people you are doing it to, that is.

6. The evil in killing X is not the harm that you do to X. X is

dead. X does not matter. It is the harm you do to Y or, if you do it right, the harm you do to everybody else. The fear, the understanding, the reminder that it could happen to them.

7. This is what makes it fun.

THE TRUTH

I could have been happy married to Mrs Findlay. I know 57 is old to start being married, but I could have coped.

I've never lived with anyone else before. Apart from my Mother. She was sick. I had to look after her. My father died when I was three. We were all alone.

Then she died. I was thirty-six. I didn't go out much. I only ever met people in the shop, which is not a good way to make friends. To meet women. No-one ever takes any notice of greengrocers. Shopkeepers in general, probably. Just give me the oranges.

There have only been four people in my life who have ever taken any interest in me, and one of them was Him, so that's really only three. There was my mother and Mrs Findlay. Gillian is very kind, too. She talks to me. I don't understand what she sees in him. She's so nice.

You learn to live with loneliness. Even He's been lonely. He's told me. It gets easy after a while. After 20 years it's second nature. Gets hard to change your ways. You get to like it. You've got your freedom.

I would have given it up for Mrs Findlay. For Betty.
Betty.
Bastard.

The SDI strategy achieved full implementation on a Saturday at the end of August, way ahead of schedule. I was becoming more efficient. I had power at last. I could feel it inside me. It was almost frightening.

I thought I might as well start in as big a way as possible, so I chose Princes Street at 11 o'clock in the morning as my venue. The streets were crowded with shoppers and tourists.

Being half a mile away, in the pub, as it happens, I didn't actually see what went on, not with my eyes, but I felt it, and am able to reconstruct the events of that morning from the eye-witness accounts carried in the papers over the next few days.

I scanned the crowds, feeling for a likely victim. I swam in between the tightly pressed swarming bodies – they seemed like ants in a nest – and I felt them. I probed, I prodded, I skimmed, until I found one I liked. There was something familiar about it. I drew on that Rage. I remembered that day, less than a week before, when I'd been standing in that very spot. I remembered the feelings I'd had. I recreated them and focused them on the body.

I went deep inside of it, and I started to push and pull. I twisted its gut. I hated it. It stopped moving forward. It dropped the bags it was carrying and stood dead still, legs apart, back arched, eyes wide open, startled and boggling. Then I crouched in my mind. I drew myself up into a tiny ball, I screamed with Rage and flung myself outwards with as much force as I could manage.

The body exploded. Its neck popped and the head shot into the air like a champagne cork. It landed upright in the gutter. The rest of the body was ripped apart by the tremendous forces I exerted from within. It was glorious. The windows of Jenner's were covered in gore. It ran down and dripped onto the pavement like rain. The people standing around the target were splashed. Some were soaked. Several slipped in the mess on the pavement. There was a leg left behind by the force of the explosion, and someone tripped over it, breaking their own arm. The splattering covered 20 square metres.

It said in the paper the next day that the person had been a post office employee. No explanation was offered for the explosion, though. The forensic people and the police couldn't find any traces of explosives. The medical types had never heard of this kind of thing happening before.

They were going to hear of it again.

It was good. Gave me a warm feeling inside. A glow of satisfaction. I finally had them worried, I was finally beginning to get somewhere. I was angry, I was starting to feel a bit more confident. I was thinking to myself, 'A few more of these and they'll realise they're really fucked.' The next one, I resolved, would happen in the Scottish Office.

THE TRUTH

He's destroyed my life.

Not just mine, either.

There's a reason he doesn't want me to go back to Betty.

He killed his own wife. Murdered her. He told me about it when we met the first time. I made him some soup and he told me he'd killed her. Pointed to the place where it happened. In his kitchen.

I'm scared of him now. Before, he was just mad. Now he's dangerous. He's different. He looks at you like he's going to hurt you. He's even different with Gillian. I've seen him snap at her. I don't know what I'll do if he ever raises his hand to her.

I'm going to the police. Next time he's away I'm calling them. They've already let him off for his wife. He told them it was an accident. Acted distraught. Pretended to have a breakdown. They had him examined by a psychiatrist. He told me. Was questioned for hours. Did tests. In the end they thought he was innocent. Accidental Death.

But I can tell them about the puppies, the bag of legs, the kittens. They won't believe he can explode people, even though he can. I'll tell them he thinks he's the Antichrist. Tell them he's sick, needs to be locked away.

I can get him taken off. Locked up. When they see what he's done they'll think he's crazy. I don't know if he is or not, but they'll think so. Show them the room with the flies. Show them this book. Tell them it's all him, even though it's my writing.

Sometimes, when I am holding seminars on the nature and practice of Evil for PISP group members, or for members of my network of evildoers, I like to talk to them in parables. Little stories which illustrate the ways in which Evil can work. This is one of them. It is an account of an incident which Meek and I were involved in some months ago, when I was just beginning my administry.

The network was, at that time, smaller than it is now, though it was even then reasonably substantial. I heard, through it, of a task which was waiting for me.

I told Meek to put her coat on, and we set out on the bus to Murrayfield, coming at last to a large town house with an attractive garden. We walked up the short gravel driveway and came to the front door. There was a brass plaque there, with the name Lazarowicz engraved on it. On my instruction, Meek rang the bell.

The Mistress of the house answered. She fell down on her knees and said, 'Are you the one they said could help?'

I nodded.

She took me by the arm and said, 'Help us, help us please. They said you could help. They said you were a master of the dark arts. Please. Have pity on us, on my poor husband in his hour of suffering. Thank God you've come. There isn't long left.'

With this, she led us up the stairs and through a door into a well-appointed bedroom. There was a built-in wardrobe running the substantial length of one wall, and a very elegant selection of natural fibre rugs lay scattered on the pine floor. On the bed lay a man. That he was in great pain was immediately apparent. There was no hiding the fact that he was in the very extremes of distress.

As we approached the bed, the man's eyes closed and a great rattling sound came from his chest. His wife broke down sobbing. 'You're too late. He's dead.'

'Never fear,' I reassured her. 'My associate here is a trained nurse.'

I told Meek to do what she could for him. She pummelled his chest, she breathed into his mouth, she massaged him, but achieved no result. After five minutes I told her to stop.

'He is, as you can see, quite dead,' I said to the mistress. 'However, it is quite possible for me to bring him back. If you want me to, that is.'

She indicated that this was, indeed, the case.

'Very well then,' I said. 'Go and stand by him and hold his hand.'

She did this. I spread out my arms and threw back my head. I intoned in a deep, booming voice, 'Arise, Lazarowicz. Arise and be as you were. Lift up your head and talk.'

Strictly speaking, none of this display was really necessary, but it is as well to make an effort with your presentation in these circumstances.

The eyes of the man who was lying on the bed began to open.

'Do you believe in me?' I asked Meek and the Mistress.

'Yes,' they both replied.

'Good,' I said. 'Then watch and see what I have done.'

The man on the bed opened his eyes fully, and then he

sat up. Then he started to scream. 'The pain, the pain, I can't bear it, make it go away.'

'There,' I said. 'I have restored him to life.'

'Is that it?' the woman asked. 'What about the pain?'

'What did you expect?' I replied.

I turned to go and bade Meek follow me. As we were crunching down the gravel drive, leaving the screaming man and his sobbing wife behind us, Meek asked me how long the man would survive.

'I don't know,' I said. 'Years, probably. In terrible pain. They won't be able to do anything for him. And they won't be able to kill him because they'll think it's immoral. It's pathetic, but it's true. Morally, we are in a much stronger position than they are.'

I turned to her and took her hand. We were laughing. 'I hope,' I said, once I'd calmed down a little, 'that you've learned something today about the Nature of Evil.'

Did you get all that down, you sprout-faced dung-head?

Good. Don't stop writing, we've got a bit more to do.

Head this next bit 'Betrayal'.

BETRAYAL

Torquil came to me last night. He had some interesting things to say to me.

First thing he did was ask a question.

'Do you know who your friends are?'

I didn't understand what he meant, so he repeated himself. I still didn't understand, and he would only repeat the question. I grew more and more frustrated until he said:

'One of them is betraying you.'

'One of whom?' I said, but he would say nothing.

I asked him again, 'Do you mean a member of my network, one of my lieutenants?' but he simply stared at me. Finally he said, 'One of them does not love you as you think they do.' Then he vanished and I was left to ponder what he had said.

He must, I reasoned, mean one of my servants. But which one? And in what way?

Meek?

No. Definitely not. She is devoted to me. She would never betray me.

I realised he probably meant Judith. She has been becoming less reliable than Meek, and she has always been stronger. She does not love me. She had never given herself over to me entirely. She could be a threat to me. She is powerful. She has taken over my duties at the Scottish Office.

I resolved to do something about her. Something bloody and painful. Still, it made me feel sad. I went back to this book to read my account of how we first met, and the great things we achieved together in the early days. Then I realised that I had never read this book before, and then I saw what you had done.

He was talking about you. Torquil was talking about you, you wormhole cunt.

No, keep writing. I want you to write this down.

I almost admire you for what you have done. That's the last nice thing I'll ever say about you. Probably the last thing I'll ever say about you full-stop. I didn't think you had it in you. What with this and your asking questions and your making overtures to Meek and your being insolent, well, you really are quite a spunky little man, aren't you?

Tough shit, though. It makes no difference.

It's no use protesting. You have betrayed me.

You, you old cunt, are fucked.

But first, the guidelines. There's only one more bit to do, then I'll be finished with them. After that I'll be finished with you too.

Guidelines on the Implementation of Evil

A note on personal attachments

1. Speaking generally, Practitioners of Evil cannot afford to form attachments to other human beings.

2. If such attachments are formed, they will generally cause some hindrance at some point, the overcoming of which will require great effort and fortitude.

3. For those who are Strong in Evil, there are, in any case, few if any who are worthy of being the objects of such an attachment.

4. By far the most convenient (and the most conducive to the facilitation of the implementation of Evil) attitude to adopt towards other human beings is one of callous indifference.

Guidelines for the Implementation of Evil

Questionnaire

We hope you have found these guidelines useful. See overleaf for further information.

It would be of great help in preparing any future edition of these guidelines if members of the network of evildoers could photocopy and complete the attached questionnaire by ticking the appropriate box(es) and return it to the chief executive through the usual channels.

I found the guidelines:

coverage
- ☐ comprehensive
- ☐ patchy

reader-friendliness
- ☐ easy to understand
- ☐ moderately easy to understand
- ☐ moderately hard to understand
- ☐ hard to understand
- ☐ incomprehensible

usefulness
- ☐ useless
- ☐ quite useful
- ☐ useful
- ☐ very useful
- ☐ extremely useful

I now think that my understanding of Evil is:

☐   complete

☐   patchy

☐   I do not understand evil

I would like to make the following suggestions of subjects for inclusion in subsequent editions:

THE TRUTH

This is the real truth. He's making me write it.

This is my confession. He says that if I write this and the next thing, and if I do it properly, I will suffer less later on.

I believe him. He can do terrible things to people. I've got to write it. I've got no choice.

My confession.

I, the Grocer, am a slimy, treacherous, piece of shit. A wart. Less than the pus in a boil. A trickle of gleet from an infected orifice.

I am worthless.

I have betrayed my Master.

I have lusted after His servant, even though he forbade it.

I have deliberately despoiled the book of His Teachings, and mocked his Guidelines for the Implementation of Evil.

I am not worthy even of being His slave. I do not deserve to live. I shall get down on my knees and beg my Master to torment me, to make me suffer, to punish me for what I have done. For I have betrayed Him when He placed His Trust in me and I should have repaid His Trust with gratitude and with devotion.

I confess, furthermore, that I am:

a dilatory cunt
a stupid, worthless, piece of shit
a pederast
a turnip-brained twat

I pray that my Master, in His Infinite Wisdom, punish

225

me justly, but that he show me, in the end, some mercy, and that I be allowed to die quickly and without suffering too much.

FINAL APPEARANCE

This is the last bit I shall be asking you to write, and I shall be watching you closely to see that you do it properly.

I trust you are recovered from the strain of writing your confession yesterday? I had not expected to see so many tears, or to be subjected to so many wailing, whining, pleas for mercy. Must have taken it out of you.

Now, write.

I got her. That withered old hag. Your special friend.

I'd been to her house, of course, so I knew where she would be. It was easy. I have killed two birds with one stone.

This is part of your punishment.

I felt her. I crawled in her left ear, sat inside her head and whispered that we should go shopping. We went. She took bags. She bought things. I don't know what. It doesn't matter. We walked down Lothian Road.

I destroyed her outside Woolworth's.

I stopped her in her tracks. I probed her with the Rage I felt for you. My will flew around her like a pack of wild dogs. The clothes were torn from her flabby, sagging, disgusting frame. I split her open. Her guts splashed out onto the pavement and lay there coiled in a steaming pile. She watched them with a stupid, surprised expression on her face. Then I tore her arms and legs off and left her writing on the pavement in a pool of blood and shit. She still had her hat on.

He's lying.

I saw that. You wrote something extra. What did you say?
    I see.
    No, I'm not lying. Here, look. Here's her head.
    Recovered? Enough to write?
    Good.
    I tossed the old witch's head into your lap like that because you didn't believe me. I was going to let you kiss it later on, but I won't now. She still looks quite attractive, don't you think, with her lipstick and her hat?
    He shat himself when I did that. When I threw him his present. He was sick. He was almost sick on the Book, but by luck or good judgement he managed to turn away and direct his flow onto the floor.
    He's still white and trembling though. I'm surprised he can write at all.
    You go and rest now for a while, little man. It's going to get a lot worse for you, and you'll need all your strength. Besides, it'll be more fun if you're stronger.

THE TRUTH

It's been a long time since He made me write that last bit down. It's been terrible. I thought he was going to kill me, but he's too clever for that. Too wicked. I thought he'd ruined my life before, but now he's ruined it more. It just goes to show what he always said. 'It will get worse, you know.' It's true. It will. It does.

I couldn't stand to think about it for months, but some of the detail is starting to get a wee bit hazy now, so maybe it's alright. Most of the physical pain has stopped. I still get the nightmares. I still see his face when I close my eyes. I'll try to tell you what happened. If it gets too much I'll stop.

He made Gillian stand in the corner and watch, to humiliate me. He said to her 'You'll enjoy this. We're going to decorate the Grocer like he decorated my book'. She said 'Leave him alone, Hector, he's harmless,' and he said 'That's hardly the point, is it?' She insisted. 'Leave him alone' and he turned to her and said 'Shut the fuck up, bitch, or you'll be next'.

He made me take my shoes, socks and trousers off and sit on the kitchen table with my back against the wall. Then he nailed my legs to the table. A nail through each shin and a nail through each thigh. He used a huge hammer and nine-inch nails. It was agony. I saw Gillian shudder with each blow of the hammer. Then he nailed my arms to the wall, a nail through each forearm and each upper arm, and then he got out some knives.

He cut my left ear off with a bread knife. It made a horrible noise, but it didn't it hurt. I think it was because I was so frightened and numb from the pain of the nails. Gillian screamed and went white. When he'd finished he showed me my ear. It was all ragged and bloody. He said, 'Obviously a bread knife isn't the right implement. I've made a bit of a pig's ear of this' and started laughing. There were tears in his eyes. Then he got out my fruit knife, the one I keep in my jacket pocket, and cut off my right ear.

He used my fruit knife to make the holes in the middle of the ears bigger, then he produced a roll of copper wire. He threaded wire through the tops of the ears and made a hook at either end. He said, 'Look, I've made you a new pair of spectacles.' He put them on and put his face close up to mine. He was grinning. He put his face close up against Gillian's. She looked sick. Then he took them off and tried to put them onto my face but they wouldn't stay so he looked at me pretending to be disappointed and stuck his bottom lip out and said, 'Oh dear, silly me, of course you've got nothing to keep these up with. Never mind,' and he stuck the ends of the wire into my face. I could feel the blood running down and dripping onto my shirt.

He looked at my shirt and said, 'Oh dear, look, your shirt's getting dirty. Let's wash that for you,' and he cut it off me so I was completely naked.

Then he said, 'What shall we do now? Nipples I think.' And he bent down and cut off my left nipple. That hurt. It was agony. It was a hot pain that went deep into my chest. He said, 'Oh, did that hurt? Hang on, don't go away. I'll get something for that,' and he reached up to the far end of the shelf over the table and got a tub of table salt and poured a pile of it onto his hand and said, 'Here, we'll rub some of this into that nasty cut and it'll make it better, you poor wee soldier, and he rubbed the salt into it and I screamed and fainted but then I came around again and he was saying, 'Don't fall asleep yet, we haven't even started yet. There's the other nipple to do, for one thing,' so he did it all over again.

When he'd cut off both the nipples he took them in his hand and said, 'What shall we do with these? . . . I know,' and he got more wire and threaded about a foot of the wire through one of them and said, 'Actually you know I think this is going to look quite pretty,' and he cut the wire and bent it over saying, 'We don't want this little chap to come off now do we?' and he pushed the end of the wire through my cheek. He said that I was going to have the wire sticking through my face like a cat's whiskers, except that my whiskers would have a nipple on either end and then he said, 'Mm, tongue as well, I think, open wide now,' and when I wouldn't he said, 'I can make you, you know,' and when I still wouldn't he went and got an axe out of the cupboard in the hall and smashed its back into my left knee and said, 'Now, your tongue, please,' so I had to open my mouth and stick out my tongue and grabbed hold of it with a pair of pliers and pulled it hard and stuck the wire through it and then he pushed the wire through my other cheek from the inside and then he said, 'Hang on a moment while we just stick the nipple on the end,' and he pushed the nipple on and stood back and said, 'There, that looks very nice. A charming effect. What next? Oh, sorry, of course you can't talk, can you? Silly of me to forget.'

Gillian said that that was enough now, you've hurt him enough, just leave him alone, but he said, 'Oh no. we've hardly started.' She was shaking and crying, big heaving sobs so he hit her, hard, across the face and sent her flying. She cracked her head on the worksurface. I think she was out cold.

He made a great show of thinking about what to do and then said, 'Fingers and toes next,' and he sighed and said, 'This is going to take forever,' and it did. He cut all my fingers and toes off, one by one, with my own knife. He put them all on pieces of wire and stuck them all into my upper body and said I looked a bit like a pin cushion, a digital pin cushion, and then he started with his laughing again.

When he'd finished he looked at me and said, 'You know, I think we're almost finished now. Just the centrepiece left to do, really,' and he suddenly picked up the axe again and smashed it down into my crotch and tore off my penis and testicles. He threaded them onto more wire and said, 'Where shall we put them?' and he suddenly smashed the axe into my nose and tore it off and shoved the wire into the hole in my face and that's the last I remember until I woke up in hospital. They told me there I'd been found by a trainload of commuters who were getting off the 7.30 from Glasgow on Monday morning in Waverley Station.

LATER

He came to see me when I was in the hospital. I can't remember when, exactly. It must have been a few months later, because he'd been in hospital himself. I haven't seen him since. Not in the flesh.

He looked strange. Different. There was a fierce light in his eyes, and he looked calmer, more confident. Gillian says that psychotics often do. He was smartly dressed and neat. Very professional looking, not at all shabby. He gave me the book and stood there looking at me. He was cold and aloof. He threw the book onto my bedside table, nodded, and turned away without speaking. There was a note pasted inside. It said

Dear Grocer
Here's your book. I realise I don't need it now,

anyway. I was only messing about when we were writing it. Pissing about in a small town when I should have been out bringing ruin and damnation to the whole planet. In a way it was a waste of time, but I was learning.

I don't need any guidelines to the implementation of evil. I am evil. You can keep them, and use them to tell your little story. I'm going to disappear from view now. I have some more suffering to do. But you know I'll be out there soon. And I'll be running things in a couple of years from now, and then . . .

For what it's worth I'm almost sorry for what I did to you. I was wrong about you, though you did betray me in your own small way. It was Judith all along. I should have seen it, with her name and everything. Judith X Heriot. It was blindingly obvious. I've written an extra something to try to explain what happened. It's on a piece of paper folded inside at the end of the book.

This is Hector's piece of paper. I think he was quite upset when he wrote it. The handwriting's all shaky.

A VISIT

That night, the night I mutilated you, I slept fitfully. Alone. Meek had gone back to her flat. I was going over what had happened, and I felt uneasy. My mind was racing. I was thinking about my job, I was thinking about you, but most of all I was thinking about Evil and how I still hadn't really achieved anything of any consequence. I'd grown. I'd discovered all the essential elements of Evil: organisation, motive, violence, but all I'd done was frighten one small town and hurt a few people and killed one or two. Maybe. My mind was racing and I wasn't even certain of that. Had I really exploded those women, or had I made it up? I didn't know. Still don't, but it doesn't matter.

I was restless, but I fell into a light sleep, and Torquil appeared. He was with a man I eventually recognised as Earl Warren, and they were discussing the assassination of J F Kennedy and the findings of the Warren Commission. I'm telling you all this detail so that it fits in with everything else I've told you, and because what happened next was so horrible. So I can put it off for a little while.

Warren was saying that, though it seemed unlikely, we had to go with Lee Harvey Oswald as the assassin because there was no more plausible alternative. Torquil's only response to this was to keep saying, 'You got the wrong man, you got the wrong man.' Warren would not listen, and Torquil kept repeating himself. Eventually Warren said he had to be off as he had business to attend to. He turned on his heel and vanished, and even as he did so, Torquil called after him, 'You got the wrong man.'

I woke up suddenly. Torquil was sitting by my bed. 'You got the wrong man,' he said. I knew he meant you. I'd had a terrible feeling I was doing you wrong even at the time. Torquil was moaning. He said, 'As if I don't have enough to do, now this. Okay, wake up, get yourself presentable, you're having a visit.'

'You,' he said, 'are in deep shit.'

I said that I thought I'd been circumspect, discreet, in all my operations. I'd had no trouble at all.

Torquil's eyes glanced upwards, and he shrugged his shoulders. 'Maybe that's the trouble,' he said. 'No trouble. Little does he know. Okay my boy, are you in for a shock now. Watch this.'

So saying, he began to shimmer, and as he did so the darkness became thicker. Darker. It became unpleasantly warm, but cold at the same time. There was thunder somewhere. And screaming. There was a flickering light, as of fire, and a billowing of smoke.

A figure appeared. A man. Quite small, but over-whelmingly compelling. Though he was only about five foot four, he seemed to fill the entire room. He had a beard. He seemed familiar, and I realised that he looked not a little like myself. He was, as far as I could tell, dressed in a three piece suit. Grey. White shirt. Pink bow tie.

The figure reached into his waistcoat pocket and took something out. A card. A business card. He handed it to me and said, 'Please read it' in a voice which commanded rather than asked. It echoed, even though there are many soft furnishings and a deep shag carpet in my bedroom and I had never heard an echo in there before.

I read the card.

'Stan?' I asked.

'Read again,' said the voice.

I did so.

I saw that I had misread the card. Then My Father spoke to me. It was the greatest night of my life. And the most terrible.

My Father told me that he had been watching my progress with interest. And with growing disappointment. He said that I seemed reluctant to take on my role as his son, as the Embodiment of Evil. He confessed to me that he had not anticipated this. He said that he, for his part, was sorry that he had not been around to visit before now, but he had been very busy with a number of other projects. But on the whole, he said, it was high time for me to get my act together. He had come, he said, to teach me a lesson.

'Your technique,' he said, 'is a little, at best, shall we say naïf, or perhaps jejune. I know that you are working with the best of intentions, and you do have a very impressive theoretical grasp of Evil, for which I must compliment you, but your practical implementation and application of all that theory is, well, pathetic. I would like, now, if I may, to give you just a few pointers or tips, just to steer you slightly in the right direction.'

He leant over me, put his face right up to mine and whispered. 'The main thing I want to say,' he said, 'is STOP PISSING ABOUT AND GET ON WITH IT.'

I've never been so frightened. He screamed at me and as he did so I heard a thousand screams in my head and my body was wracked with such pain. I think that even you, after all I did to you, could hardly imagine the pain I felt. He talked to me as he was hurting me. He said that he would make it last a thousand years, even though it was only one night. I had to suffer to know true Evil. I had to know pain to become less ordinary, less humdrum. If I were to rule over the common herd I'd have to have a reason, a purpose, so he was going to give me one by filling my life with pain. I was already tortured, but now . . . Then he said, 'I'm doing this mainly to get the Edinburgh out of you. You're so narrow-minded. Why did I make you Scottish? Someone from any other town, any other country, would already be ruling the entire planet, but not you. Edinburgh's the centre of the whole universe, isn't it? NO, IT ISN'T. Forget Edinburgh. Forget Edinburgh you parochial little bastard. Forget Scotland and discover the world at your feet.'

I won't start to describe what he did to me. There are no words. It lasted forever. It was agony. I have been to hell. I'm still there.

I have realised that I got it all wrong. You can't be evil in Edinburgh. It isn't the whole world, even though I was always brought up to believe it was. It's too small. You can't be evil and parochial. It doesn't work. I'm going to have to try much, much harder. It's going to hurt me as much as it hurts anyone else. I'm not even sure that I want to do it. I just have to.

You were kind to me. I'm sorry. In a way.

HELEN

This is what he had told me about his wife. Helen, she was called. From what I know of her she sounded really nice. I saw the photo he had of her. He carried it around in his wallet. Dark hair, long and curly. Big eyes, blue. Pale skin, freckles. Very pretty.

I tell you this now because I notice that he's started talking about it in public, making out that it's a great tragedy. I wasn't going to mention it. It seemed so pathetic. A silly story. But now I've seen a few magazine articles where he's gone on about it, and what a terrible accident it was, and how it nearly drove him to despair and suicide. It always gets him a big write up. And aye, the bit about the suicide attempts and despair might be true, but if it is, he's well over it, let me tell you, and he's just using it to get your sympathy.

It was in the kitchen that he told me. Just a couple of weeks after we first met. It was difficult to make some of what he said out because he was crying so much when he told me. Anyway, as near as I can remember, this is what he said:

'I did not murder her. I killed her. No-one said it was murder. I didn't do anything wrong.

'We were playing one of those games you play when you're married, or before you're married. A courting ritual. Before the foreplay. Fooling about.

'We were throwing food at each other in the kitchen. There was a lot of food around because we had just been to the supermarket. She had started it by flicking chocolate raisins at me. I had retaliated with a soft morning roll, which hit her on the head. She replied, laughing and retreating to the back wall, under the shelf on which we'd been stacking the tins we'd bought, with one of the cream cakes we were going to have with our tea when we'd finished unpacking the shopping. It hit me in the face, and the cream dribbled down my chin. She laughed even more. I said something like 'right, you cow, now you die'.

'I said it as a joke, but that was what happened. She had squealed with delight because she knew she was going to get walloped with a cake or something. I looked around for a missile and found a plum, a soft, over-ripe one. I threw it, gently, but it went high. It hit a large tin of cling peaches that was balanced on top of two other tins on the edge of the shelf. The tin fell off and hit her on the head. She died.

'I watched it fall. I tried to call out, but there wasn't time, even though it seemed to be happening in slow motion. I watched it hit her. I watched her fall to the floor. I saw her die.'

He was trembling all over when he told me all this. It took him ages to get the words out. There were tears running down his cheeks and onto his shirt, snot bubbling out of his nose. He kept sniffing it up.

He told me that the police found him cradling her head in his arms. He thought he must have called them himself, though he had no memory of doing so. They were sympathetic. They never accused him of any crime.

The office gave him time off work, to rest and recuperate. Two months. Then he went back to work, he said, and acted as if everything was normal, and that was when he realised he was the Antichrist.

He said he realised now that the plum had been guided by Satan. That it was meant to be. That his father intended this to be the start of his journey into Evil. Didn't stop him from crying, though.

Peaches, by the way, were her favourite fruit. Peaches was what he had called her.

SOMETHING I'VE PASTED IN

I'm pasting this thing in here because it tells the story better than I could. I got it from a friend who works at the Royal Edinburgh hospital. You know who she is. She's sitting here with me now, writing this down as I dictate it. I can't write very fast. It hurts too much.

It's been hard for her. She loved Him. He hurt her, and then He left her.

She brought these things to me the other day. She stole them from a filing cabinet at the hospital because if they were left there they'd never see the light, and one day they might be important. They're supposed to be confidential, but they're important in the light of what's happening now. They'll tell you what happened to Him after he did what he did to me. I think it was later on that day, I think the dates match up. Maybe it was the next day. It's a bit difficult to tell. No matter.

Report to the Mental Welfare Commission

Mr Hector Sextus Hepton of 34 Regent Terrace, Edinburgh, was detained by Sergeant Thomas McCall and WPC Amanda Cornwall of the Lothian and Borders Police at 11.17 on 24th Sept in Princes St Gardens under Section 117 of the Mental Health (Scotland) Act 1984. Sergeant McCall and WPC Cornwall had been alerted by an associate of Mr Hepton, Ms Judith Heriot, who expressed her concern to them that Mr Hepton was behaving in a manner she described as 'psychotic'. Ms Hepton accompanied the officers to the scene and identified Mr Hepton.

At the time of his detention Mr Hepton was running through the gardens catching pigeons. A number of headless birds were found about his person. There was no trace of the heads. Upon being cautioned and advised of his rights, Mr Hepton said 'So, you have come at last. Stop pissing about and get on with it'. He then asked if Ms Heriot could accompany them as he felt he needed a friendly face. Ms Heriot looked apprehensive but agreed when assured that she would be accompanied by the officers.

Mr Hepton was then escorted to the waiting police vehicle. Getting into the vehicle he said 'I shall arise again, more powerful than you could possibly imagine'.

Mr Hepton was taken to a place of safety as
defined under the terms of the Act, this being
the Royal Edinburgh Hospital. He was accompanied
to an examination room by Ms Heriot. On arrival
he was examined by a doctor and Mental Health
Officer and further detained for 72 hours under
Section 24 of the Act for further evaluation.

AJC (WPC)

Social Circumstances Report
Mental Health (Scotland) Act 1984

Name: Hector Sextus Hepton   **D.O.B.** 06.06.65
Address: 34 Regent Terrace, Edinburgh
Nearest Relative: none
Hospital: Royal Edinburgh
Responsible Medical Officer: Prof Gilles Alexander
GP: not known
Mental Health Officer: Mr Neil Watt
Date of Hospital Admission: 24th Sept

Details of Compulsory Detention this Episode:
   Initial detention under Section 117 of the Mental Health (Scotland) Act 1984. Further detained under Section 24 of the Act at 12.32pm 4th September.

Basis of Report
Mr Hepton is a man of excellent character who has, over the past few years, had a number of distressing episodes of mental ill-health which have recently forced him to resign his post as a senior administrator at the Scottish Office. He has a private income, and lives in the family home in Regent Terrace, next-door to the American Consulate.

Family History:
Mr Hepton has no surviving family. His parents were killed in a boating accident when he was

14, after which he was brought up by his paternal grandmother, now also dead. He had no brothers or sisters, and there is no trace of any other surviving blood-relatives. He was married for ten years, but his wife was killed in a domestic accident some eighteen months previously to the current episode.

Previous Involvement with Psychiatric Services:
Mr Hepton has been an out-patient at the Professorial Unit of the Royal Edinburgh Hospital for four years. Prof Gilles Alexander has taken a personal interest in his case, having been at school with Mr Hepton's father, and being of the opinion that Mr Hepton's case presents a number of points of interest. Mr Hepton's condition worsened considerably upon the death of his wife 18 months previous to the current admission, since when he has been on a substantial course of medication designed to counteract his delusional tendencies.

Circumstances leading to current admission:
Mr Hepton was detained by the constabulary in Princes St Gardens. He was in a highly distressed state. He had been catching and mutilating pigeons and was using obscene and threatening behaviour towards members of the public in the Gardens. The Arresting Officers, who had been summoned to the scene by Ms Judith Heriot, a friend of Mr Hepton who said that she was worried about the harm he might do to himself or someone

else, detained him under Section 117 of the Act and brought him to the Royal Edinburgh, where he was examined by Prof Alexander and the Mental Health Officer on duty. Ms Heriot accompanied Mr Hepton to the Royal Edinburgh at Mr Hepton's request. Upon examination he informed Prof Alexander and the MHO that he was the Antichrist and exhibited aggressive behaviour, despite having, until then, maintained friendly relations with Prof Alexander whom he had known all his life, the Professor being a family friend. It was decided that Mr Hepton should be placed in secure accommodation in the Intensive Psychiatric Care Unit. He was formally advised of his rights and detained under Section 24 of the Act at 12.32pm. He was then escorted to the IPCU, again with Ms Heriot who, in the view of the MHO and Prof Alexander, was a calming influence on him.

View of the Individual under Detention:
Mr Hepton has been unable to formulate any coherent view of his current circumstances. It is his belief that he is the embodiment of evil, and will advance no statement other than that he is the antichrist and has been put on the earth in order to implement a reign of terror on behalf of his father, Satan.

MHO's Conclusion and Care Plan:
Mr Hepton is in a highly distressed condition and, whilst this remains the case, presents

a potential danger both to himself and to the community. It is my belief that he should remain in care for at least another 28 days, and am therefore recommending that an application be made within the 72-hour period permitted by Section 24 of the Act, for a further compulsory detention order under Section 26 of the Act. In my view this recommendation is true both to the letter and the spirit of the Act.

Neil Watt, MHO. 24 Sept, 13.06.

Well, that was two or three or four years ago. I've not been very well. It took a long time just to get to the point where I could think again. Think about what happened. Now I'm a bit frightened. I'm keeping my head down in case He decides to come looking for me. I'm not letting this book out of my sight, just in case.

In the Bible there's that bit at the end where that guy sees four horsemen coming, and they're bringing the apocolypse with them. Well I've seen the Apocolypse coming too. I saw it on television. It wasn't riding horses, it was just sitting there, chatting all amiable with Kirsty Wark on Newsnight. I used to write His words down.

To think that for ages I thought He was just mad. I must have been mad. So did the people at the Hospital, mind. Obviously. They thought he was barking. You can tell that from the reports. On the other hand, Gillian always knew there was something about Him, otherwise she wouldn't have loved Him. She's scared too now. Very.

They let him go, of course. From the hospital. They had to. They can't keep you locked up just for thinking that you're the embodiment of evil. Not if you're rational and you don't shite your breeks and don't go for anyone with a kitchen knife. He's way too clever for that. Gillian says he was only in there for a couple of weeks and then they discharged him with some medication. She says there was a remarkable turn-around in his behaviour while he was in there. Came out all composed.

And that was the last either of us ever saw of him, in person, anyway.

About a year after he was detained, there was a big rally at the end of Princes Street protesting about the break-up of the United Kingdom. I've always been in favour of it myself, so I didn't pay it much mind. Until, that is, I saw that one of the speakers addressing the crowd was Himself. He got on the telly. Got interviewed in the papers. I don't know how he got himself into that position, exactly, but he seemed to be doing alright at it. Mind you, he'd always been hanging about with those politician types. There were always a few of them at those little dos at his house. I'd only remembered there being SNP types, but he must have been hanging about with the other lot too.

A few months later there was a general election. This is the odd thing, considering how much work he'd done on the new parliament and everything, but he was standing as candidate in Eastwood, near Glasgow. For the Conservative and Unionist Party, no less. I suppose that it's easy enough to get yourself taken up as a candidate when you've got the family connections and everything, but I was shocked when I saw him on the news at the start of the campaign. He'd been all Edinburgh this, Edinburgh that before. I was even more shocked when I heard what he was saying. He spent all his time saying that the Scottish Parliament was a bad thing, and what was needed was strong central government with a strong and charismatic leadership. The only way we would ever survive and prosper in the world was as part of something big, he said. The United Kingdom. Europe. We didn't want to mess about in a tiny nation running our own affairs, he said. We weren't just parochial and provincial – we wanted to be major players. If we were strong and resolute, Scotland could have a voice, not just in the UK, but in the whole of Europe. Why, with the right leadership, there was no reason why there should not one day be a Scottish president of the European Union.

It was all 'strong leadership'. You got the feeling that he knew who he was talking about. There was a definite glint in his eye.

He went down very well with all the middle class wifies in Eastwood. They always go for that sort of thing. He was the first Tory elected in Scotland for years.

So, now he's a minister at the Treasury in London. Very strong on closer links with Europe. Very pro European Monetary Union. Seems He's managed to get the whole Tory party behind Him on that issue. Nobody's batted an eyelid at the fact it's only taken him a few months to get himself into this position. He's already being tipped as a potential Prime Minister. Of course, you know how he's managed all this – he's got himself a new network of MPs and journalists. He'll still have his contacts in the civil service up here, and more in London, I suppose.

I've seen him on TV. He's very good at it. Gave a very good interview a few months ago on mental illness and the need for people with a history of mental illness to be integrated into society. Having suffered bouts of severe depression himself he thought that this should be a priority, he said. Well, he knows how to say all the right things. Knows how to get them going. He's turned into a bit of a rabble rouser. I suppose that was always the way he was going to get what he wanted.

He's not mad. He's clever. I'm the mad one. Look at what I've done, what I let him do to me.

I'm scared. That's why I'm hiding. That's why I keep this book with me and never let it out of my sight, in case He finds out I've still got it and have written about Him.

He's powerful. He could find me in seconds if He thought about it. I hope He's forgotten all about His Grocer of Doom. I'll be very quiet. I don't want to get exploded, like he did to those women.

He was Evil even when He thought He was being pathetic. It wasn't the things he was doing – they were just bad. No, it was his motives. Something deep inside himself. He was just trying to find a way to express himself, that's all. Maybe he was being evil with a small 'e', but He would say what he was doing back then wasn't really evil at all. He always said real Evil is to do with government and power and organising things, like Hitler or someone. Oh aye, you need a special touch and all that, you need to be really warped, and most people just can't do it. You need vision too, ideas, and systems, and a crowd of other people. Well, He's got himself bigger horizons now. Good news for him. Bad news for everyone else. This is just the beginning, too. It's going to get much worse.

Hang on, there's someone at the door.

GENESIS

Very interesting. I like what you have written about me. You did especially well in that last bit in which you explain the nature of Evil. I could have put it a great deal better myself. It's quite simple. I've started using a formula to explain it. $E=M(PO)$. Evil equals malevolence multiplied by power times organisation. You would never have thought of that though, not in a million years.

Now. Write this down.

This is the beginning.

I am the capital E Evil capital O One. You are lower case n nothing. A chronicler. These are my works. Read them and weep.

Soon I shall have earthly power, and shall wield it without mercy. You shall sit at the foot of my throne and worship me amid the terrible darkness. I will prop you up on pillows and laugh at you when you fall over. Your ugly and mutilated body will remind all who see of my Power and my Will.

Hear me laugh. HA HA HA HA HA HAAA. Yes, write that down too. It's my evil laugh. I have perfected it. Chilling, isn't it? Puts the wind right up the party workers, I can tell you. I love watching them scuttle around, doing my bidding. They wouldn't do that in the SNP you know. Or even Labour. God it's great being a Tory. I don't know why I didn't think of it years ago.

Come, let us go now. There is work to be done. There is a reign of Evil to begin. You shall record it, that others might know me in my dark majesty. You can have your old room back. I shall buy you a specially adapted word-processor. It will hurt you to type, but we all have our crosses to bear. I too am wracked with pain. I think I may have a kidney infection, but I shall not let it stop my Reign of Cruelty.

This is the beginning. A mighty melon tree is growing from the evil seeds I have planted. Soon there will be a bitter harvest. The melons of evil are huge and juicy, but they are rank and full of poison.

There will be no other fruit.

There will be no need for grocers.

Perhaps the world will thank me for this. I do not care. In any case, they will be too busy suffering to notice.

Let the misery commence.